Hell's Kitten

PADDLE CREEK DADDIES BOOK FIVE

HJ WELCH

Trigger Warning

This book features frequent mentions of Jessie's mom's battle with cancer. She is in remission, but some readers might find the references to her struggles distressing.

CHAPTER 1

Jessie

In hindsight, this is probably going to be one of those funny stories I tell. Largely because this is entirely my fault.

But right now, it's the most unfunny thing I've ever experienced in my twenty-three years of life.

"Jessie?" my boyfriend, Parker, says in surprise as he opens the door to his apartment. No. Not in surprise. In horror. "What are you doing here?"

My stomach threatens to drop, but I always stubbornly cling to hope and optimism even when disaster is staring me in the face. It worked when my mom was diagnosed five years ago, and it's going to damn well work now. My boyfriend *is* excited to see me. He just doesn't realize it yet.

"I start classes next week, remember?" I say cheerfully. "You said I could stay with you."

His eyes widen as his gaze falls to the large suitcase on wheels sitting next to me. It's covered in various cat stickers, so there's no missing that it's mine. "I said you could come over whenever," he said slowly. "Like usual." I can't stop the dread that's pooling in my stomach. His eyes are still wide, and he's breathing pretty heavily.

He's not the only one.

Okay, so, yeah. Normally, I message him beforehand, and we make plans for me to visit over the weekend or whatever. We've been dating for a couple of years ever since he swung by Cincinnati that time and we matched on one of the apps. He sometimes visited me in the city, but with me living at home and Mom's illness, it made sense for me to come here more often than not. I know the drive with my eyes closed, and his apartment feels like home as well.

Or at least it did until about thirty seconds ago.

"Are you moving in?" Parker splutters. He makes it sound like an accusation, and he's still glaring at my suitcase like it's a bomb about to go off. I try not to think of all the rest of my stuff in my car outside.

"Uhh…" I say, feeling my cheeks heat up. "I thought you said I could stay once I started school?"

I'm rapidly feeling like a complete and utter fool. When it was clear that my mom's cancer was clearing up and I could finally start living my life again, coming to Paddle Creek to be with Parker seemed like the obvious choice. Sure, the town is kind of a dump, and the college is hardly Ivy League, but what does that matter when I'm in love?

This was supposed to be my second chance. I adore my mom and don't regret one second I dedicated to her care or a single cent I put toward her treatment. But I can't lie. It was pretty devastating giving up my cheerleading scholarship to Northern Kentucky University and watching all my friends leave town.

But now I'm here, and crashing with Parker means I can afford to get my degree. I'm all enrolled. This is happening.

So why is he looking at me like I'm a complete stranger?

"I never said you could come *live* with me, Jesus," he says, shaking his head. He's clinging to the door like it's propping him up. He's only opened it a foot or so, like he's using his body as a shield to stop me from barging in. "I know you mentioned college, but you didn't say anything about our arrangement changing. What the hell, man?"

I wince. He knows I hate it when he calls me 'man,' but he always seems to forget. Just like how he's apparently forgotten telling me that he'd take care of me and that I shouldn't worry about a thing. Was he even *listening* when we made these plans?

When *I* made these plans, I guess.

There's only so much my natural positivity can cling to when faced with the horrible, dawning realization of what's going on here.

He doesn't want me to move in with him.

I know we only see each other every couple of months, but that was why this was so exciting. It was going to be the next phase in our relationship! Doesn't he want that?

"Uh, s-sorry," I stutter, not sure what else to say. "I must have misunderstood. It's okay. I can maybe see if there are some dorm rooms left or something…"

The community college isn't big, so they don't have much accommodation as they expect people to commute from home. There might be a cheerleading house, but I'm not even on the team yet. I have to try out, and after five years I'm pretty rusty. But there's got to be a solution if I look hard enough. I can get a part-time job to pay for rent. Sure, I wasn't factoring that in when planning my finances and justifying college at all, but I'm kind of committed now.

"You're enrolled at Paddle Creek?" he says, still sounding incredulous.

Finally, I go from feeling shocked to angry. "Yes," I snap back, equally incredulous. "I came here to be with you. I'm doing this for us. I didn't text ahead because I thought it would be fun to surprise you, but clearly, I'm mistaken. What's going on, Parker? Don't you want to be with me?"

He just stares at me for a few seconds, his mouth hanging open like a goldfish.

Then a voice comes from behind him.

"What's going on, babe? Everything all right?"

And then the door opens up all the way and a man I've never seen before in my life slips his arm around my boyfriend's waist, kisses his neck, and looks at me with a frown.

Now I'm the one with the slack jaw.

"Who are you?" he asks bluntly.

"Who are *you?*" I practically shriek.

"Fuck," Parker mutters under his breath.

I'm feeling lightheaded as I look at them both. This other guy is muscly, like Parker. They both have that 'I could definitely be straight' vibe going on that I've subtly been trying to help Parker work on. I thought I could open his mind, especially now we were supposed to be living together.

I've obviously thought a great number of things that were totally and completely wrong.

"I'm Zane," the other guy says.

His gaze lingers on my kitty stickers. Then it travels over my backpack, which is slung over one shoulder and the headphones that pretty much live around my neck if they're not on my head. Both of these things have adorable cat ears, and the bag even has whiskers printed on the flap.

Normally, I'm loud and proud about my feline obsession. It's as integral to me as my sexuality and gender identity. But in that moment, I'm made to feel so small and stupid that I'd have given almost anything for plain luggage and accessories.

"I can explain," Parker is saying. I look up and realize he's not talking to me.

He's talking to Zane.

It's the final nail in the coffin. I'm still devastated, but right then I stop trying to deny what's become painfully obvious.

"I was never your boyfriend," I say softly, tears pooling in my eyes. "I was your bit on the side. *He's* your boyfriend."

Zane looks murderous as he takes his arm off Parker's waist and scowls at him. "You've been fucking this little twink behind my back? You into girls now instead of men?"

His insult slices through my already broken heart. I love my body, especially when I'm training hard and get really toned. I love being fem and all kitteny. I could work out my whole life and I'd never be as big and masc as they are. I don't even *want* that. But it hurts to be attacked for something that's not even within my control.

"No, baby!" Parker cries in distress. "It was just a bit of fun, you know? Something for a change. I'm so sorry! It meant nothing! I love you!"

Zane huffs, balling up his fists and storming back inside the apartment.

Parker goes after him, letting the door swing shut without even so much as a glance in my direction.

I stand in the hallway like a lemon, not quite believing what just happened. How can my entire world have fallen around my ankles in a matter of minutes? Was I ever going to see Parker again? I thought we were building a life together.

How long have he and Zane been a thing? Surely, Zane can't live here, or I would have seen some trace of him before now. How has Parker been keeping us apart—in real life, let alone online? I guess he doesn't have any social media accounts. He always called my Instagram posts vain and attention seeking. I told myself he was just teasing, but…

Oh my god. He probably *does* have social media. He just told me he didn't so I couldn't tag him.

I never met his friends or his family. Most of the time, we

just stayed at his place and fucked. I was so completely wrapped up in Mom's chemo appointments and taking care of her, our home, and our finances that I probably didn't think on it all half as much as I should have.

I've been a complete, gullible moron.

Come to think of it, how much *did* I talk to him about me moving in with him? I was planning on maybe getting a weekend job and contributing towards bills. I'm not a free-loader. But part of what was so nice about visiting him was that he just took charge and sorted everything. He made plans and paid for food and allowed me to switch my brain off and be pampered for a while after giving all my time and energy to my mom.

I know I definitely told him I was going to college because he said that was great news, and we celebrated by getting a pizza delivered and…having sex.

Did I tell him I'd applied to Paddle Creek? That I got in? It's not exactly a hard college to gain attendance to, but…

Oh dear. I know I told Mom everything. She'd been excited for me. She always said she liked Parker. Or at least liked the sound of him. She never met or spoke to him, after all. And I never confided any of my doubts about him to her because I was so determined that everything would be fine once she got better, and I could live my life for myself again.

But I've been walking around in a fantasy land.

I stare at Parker's door and realize in a sudden rush how many blanks I'd been filling in for this relationship. Deep down, I must have worried that he might not have been totally down for going from seeing each other once every couple of months to every day. That's why I convinced myself he'd enthusiastically agreed to live together.

This had only ever been a fling to him. When I told him I was going to college, he probably thought that meant me moving further away, not closer. I bet he was planning on using it as an easy excuse to break up with me without Zane ever finding out.

There's a small, petty part of me that's getting some savage satisfaction from knowing that I've exposed Parker's dirty little secret—a.k.a. me—to Zane. The guy might have been a douche to me, but no one deserves to be cheated on. Perhaps Parker will go from two boyfriends to none by the end of the day.

My schadenfreude only goes so far, though. I don't get so much joy out of Parker's misfortune that I want to hang around and see any more of it. It's time I start looking after myself again.

Rubbing my chest with one hand and nibbling my thumbnail on the other, I try my best to breathe. I'm still enrolled in college. I still have my car and all my stuff. I don't have much money in the bank as I gave most of it to my mom while she's still applying for a new job of her own. But I'm a hard worker. I held down *three* jobs at one point to make sure Mom and I didn't go under. I'll be okay.

And if I have to sleep in my car for the time being, well… it's still a roof over my head.

Right?

CHAPTER 2
Nim

Usually, everyone in O'Toole's knows better than to bother me.

Usually.

"Well, what have you got there?" a chipper voice asks by my shoulder. I'm sitting at the bar in the pub, minding my own business with my pint of Guinness. No one was supposed to look so closely they'd see the inside of my leather jacket. More specifically, they weren't supposed to pay attention to the tabby kitten currently asleep in my pocket.

Glancing over my shoulder, I'm mildly surprised to see Sheriff Chancey smiling warmly at me, her eyes looking hopeful of another glimpse of fluff.

I grunt and go back to my pint. The little one needs warmth and round-the-clock feeding. I've got plenty of milk for him back at home. I just wanted to swing by for a drink at the town's only gay bar before spending the rest of the evening alone.

Only gay *pub*, I should say. There's that loud and shiny bar that the kids go to in the town center where they can rub against each other with sugary cocktails and perky pop music blasting.

Not my scene.

I like peace and quiet. Sheriff Chancey is currently imposing the opposite on me.

"Ohh, what a sweetie," she says with a grin. "You're so good with all those kitties, aren't you?"

I try not to wince. If she's talking about the cats that live in my café until they can find their forever homes, then, yes. I think I am pretty good with them.

If she's talking about a completely *different* kind of kitten…no. I haven't had the best of luck with those over the years.

The pub isn't all that busy, but Donna, the dyke who runs the joint sure took her time with the customer she was serving before coming to my rescue. I think she enjoys watching me squirm. If I didn't love her like a sister, I might hate her. She knows she's safe, though, as evident from her smirk as she saunters over to us on the other side of the bar.

"Paula," she says happily, slapping her hands down on the counter. "It's been a while. How are the kids?"

The sheriff snorts. "Not kids. Teens." She shudders. "Timothy will only answer to 'TJ' now and insists he doesn't need to do his homework anymore because he's a 'major TikTok influencer.'" She uses air quotes and rolls her eyes. "I keep telling him that a thousand views isn't enough to quit the day job. And Mary-Beth refuses to ever leave her room, but when she does, it's only to hunt down *another* computer to break apart and put back together again. I wouldn't mind if she sold the ones that she fixes, but she insists she needs them all for making codes or something. My house only has so much space, you know? I swear if she's hacking into the Pentagon, it's me who's going to jail." She jerks her thumb at me. "I should have stuck with cats."

I grunt in agreement. People—especially ones you're related to—aren't worth it. They'll only mess you up, one way or another.

Donna cackles, however. "God bless you, hon. You're a trooper. What can I get you?"

Now, I know that Donna hasn't missed the fact that Chancey is in uniform. That's her way of asking her what she's *doing* here. Sure enough, the sheriff taps her badge.

"Afraid I'm on duty, Dee. Actually, my visit is official, not social."

Donna arches an eyebrow. "That so?" she says as she wipes her spotless bar down with a rag.

Chancey sighs. "Got an anonymous report of some… unsavory business taking place on the premises."

"My liquor license is up to date, officer," Donna says coldly.

Chancey holds up her hands. "I know that. That's not what the complaint was about. Someone's got their panties in a twist talking about drugs and hookers."

Seeing as I was actively nursing my stout and trying not to get involved, the laugh I bark out possibly startles me more than either of them. Donna snaps her fingers my way all the same.

"What the big man said. The most anarchy you're likely to get around here is fellas debating the merits of Hendrix over Zeppelin."

"Dunno," I say, catching her eye and feeling my mouth quirk. "It got pretty heated when some of the guys were comparing cupcake recipes the other week."

Usually, I'm a man of few words. But O'Toole's is like a second home to me since I moved to this little town a couple of years ago. I tend to stick to my café and my apartment above it. But my second love after my cats is my Harley, and there's a surprising number of bikers that congregate here.

Officially, the group goes by the Cardinals after the state bird that can be found in abundance in these parts. But more often than not, people just refer to us as the bikers or the chapter. Some are queer like me and Donna. Some aren't. They sure help to keep away anyone who might be looking for trouble either way.

I'm protective of this pub. I don't like the idea of anyone talking shit about it or the people who come here.

Chancey sighs again and shakes her head. "I know, I know," she says. "I got eyes. I know you all. It's bullshit. But you know how Mayor Durham is starting his reelection campaign, and I guess he just wants to make sure everything's in order. He asked me personally to check the situation out, and now I have." She sweeps her hand out, encompassing the few people in the pub tonight and bowing her head.

Donna hums disapprovingly as I grit my teeth. I've only seen Lyle Durham a couple of times, usually when he's cutting a ribbon or kissing babies. But he came into Toe Beans once without warning me and made a big deal of ordering a coffee before petting a cat, all while making sure several cameras were capturing every moment. He flashed me a big smile briefly, but then when he was done, he walked out without a second glance, letting his aide pay for the coffee.

He gives me the creeps. I'm big enough and ugly enough that I'm rarely physically intimidated. But a guy like that with deep pockets and powerful friends scares the shit out of me. They don't care about the little guy. They only want to get ahead, no matter who they have to step onto do it.

Donna frowns. "I thought Durham was running unopposed, wasn't he? Why does he need to do anything at all?"

"Not anymore," Chancey says. "Maurice Sanchez has thrown his hat in the ring."

"The high school principal?" Donna asks.

"Former principal," Chancey corrects. "He's not very flashy, but he's solid, dependable. A lot of folks know and trust him. I guess Durham wants to make a big song and dance about cutting down crime or something to keep their votes."

"Anything I should be worrying about, Sheriff?" Donna asks as she folds her buff and tattooed arms. She's got lines around her eyes as she narrows them, but anyone who mistakes her age for weakness instead of wisdom is an idiot.

Chancey shrugs. It's interesting to me how both women are white and blonde, but Paula looks like she'd give you a hug if you skinned your knee, whereas Donna would probably make you knock back a shot of vodka and then get the hell on with it.

"Honestly?" the sheriff says. "I'm not sure. It could have been a genuine complaint. Let's just say I'm going to see if we get any more anonymous tips over the next couple of weeks. If Durham's trying to clean the town up, there are plenty of other places he could be looking that aren't minority spaces."

Some of the tension in my chest eases. This might be nothing. It might be the start of something bad. But it's good to know that our sheriff isn't one to be played, and that she has our backs.

The mayor and his rich boy club could do a lot of good in this rundown town. The reason I was able to buy my property and set up my business was because the real estate value is so low in these parts. Everything except the football stadium is practically falling apart. Word on the street is that the town is mostly owned by a guy called McKenna—one of Durham's pals. But he sure seems to like snatching up opportunities from folks then just sitting on them.

It's not my place to think about politics. I don't care for it. They're all crooked schmucks. I like to take care of my own corner of the world, and right now, that means getting the little bundle of fluff home before he can start wriggling too much and causing a fuss. He needs his dinner and so do I.

"Thank you for the heads-up, Paula," Donna says as I take a final mouthful of Guinness, leaving the glass half-full as I stand.

Chancey smirks. "I don't know what you're talking about, Dee. I just came to look for drugs and hookers. You lot have a nice night, now."

Donna and I both watch as the sheriff walks out, tipping her hat to a couple of the guys who look her way from the pool table.

"What do you make of all that?" Donna asks me.

I shrug and grunt, flicking my eyes her way. "Not good," I say simply.

I'm not a particularly optimistic person. The world is full of bad people who like to hurt others to make themselves feel powerful. There are plenty of good folks as well, don't get me wrong. But in my experience, kindness has a way of getting punished.

Best to keep your head down and watch out for your own, I find. So that means that, yeah, I might find myself coming down to O'Toole's a little more often over the next few weeks to watch out for trouble. If Durham knows what's good for him, he won't make a platform out of trampling on queer people. I'd like to think that in this day and age, that wouldn't be the sort of thing that gets votes.

But I also own a TV, and I know that can be *exactly* the kind of issue that wins bigots over.

Something tells me trouble is on its way.

I just hope it doesn't fall right into my lap.

CHAPTER 3

Jessie

It turns out that sleeping in your car is about as fun as it sounds.

But I'm not about to waste money on a hotel, even if Paddle Creek does have a very fun-looking nautical-themed motel called Sunken Treasure. Their rates are pretty low, but they're not free. I need to save every cent I can to afford a deposit on an apartment.

My first move was reaching out to the college administration office. However, they said they wouldn't be able to help me until classes start next week when they'd know if anyone has dropped out and doesn't need their room anymore. Even then, there are apparently people ahead of me on the list, so there's no guarantee if or when I'd get a place.

I can't face the uncertainty, so I spent yesterday afternoon emailing Realtors about vacancies but so far, no one has gotten back to me.

Rather than worrying myself silly about it, I'm focusing my efforts this morning on job hunting. I still look kind of put together despite a truly awful night's sleep, worrying constantly that I was going to wake up to find someone staring at me or—worse—someone breaking into the car.

But I was able to brush both my hair and teeth and apply fresh deodorant, so I feel reasonably presentable. I'm hoping to be able to get a day pass to use the showers at a gym, but for now, I'm confident enough to walk into places and see if anyone's hiring.

I've basically been working my way down Main Street. I don't know my schedule yet, but I'm really hoping I can get a weekend shift somewhere and maybe something during the week if my classes allow it. Retail seems like the obvious choice for flexible hours, but so far, no one has any openings.

In fact, half the buildings on this street are boarded up. Has it gotten worse since I last visited? I guess Parker never brought me around these parts—probably in case anyone saw us. *Urgh.* But…yeah. I didn't appreciate the town was this dilapidated.

Why the hell did I move here again? I curse myself for the millionth time as I nibble my thumbnail. I really did think I was in love with that asshole. But even after only twenty-four hours I'm starting to understand that I was just wrapped up in the *idea* of Parker more than the man himself. I thought my heart would be aching with how much I miss him. But mostly, I'm just furious. More at myself than him, funnily enough.

And now I'm stuck in this dead-end town, trudging from shop to shop as my hope of finding something today dwindles. I'm starting to feel truly despondent when I look ahead a few stores, and my heart skips a beat. *Of course!* How could I have forgotten that Paddle Creek has a cat café? Parker always promised he'd take me there, but obviously he didn't. It's clear to me now how embarrassed he was with my cat obsession, let alone wanting to avoid us being seen in public, but I don't care what he thinks anymore.

Cats are amazing, and Toe Beans looks like the most perfect place in the world to work. Hell, that wouldn't be a chore. That would be awesome.

"Please have a vacancy, please, please," I whisper to myself as I bounce up to the front door. Unlike most of the other businesses I've been into this morning, the café is jammed despite the fact that it's a Wednesday. I peer through the glass and see all the mismatched furniture with lacy table coverings and teapots.

Oh my god, it's *adorable*.

This is the place for me. I just know it. I've still got my cat-ear headphones around my neck and my cat-face backpack on. I look perfect for the part! I don't care what kind of work I'll have to do. I'll wash the dishes, sweep the floors, I'll even clean out the litter boxes. It's clear to me that this will be good for my poor, wounded soul.

The first ray of sunshine in the downpour that has become my life.

As I stop ogling through the glass and actually make my way inside, a little bell jingles above my head. The line is almost to the door, and seeing as I don't want to buy anything, I could probably just skip it. But that feels rude, so instead I wait my turn.

There's plenty to look at in the meantime. All along the walls are different-sized shelves for the cats to move around the room, not to mention several rope bridges. There are hammocks and softly lined boxes and so many scratching posts.

Then there are the kitties themselves. It's hard to count them, but I'd guess there are about twenty milling around. Some are sleeping, some are wandering, and some are playing with customers. I notice there are two people wearing T-shirts with the café's name on them, standing at either end of the coffee shop, observing the cats. When a small child gets a bit too enthusiastic and attempts to put a poor ginger baby in a headlock, the staff member is there in a flash, gently helping the child and their parents to respect the cat's boundaries.

I'm impressed. I've always wondered about the ethics of establishments like this. But it seems these people's jobs are purely looking out for feline welfare. Combine that with the big, pretty signs on the wall saying that all cats are looking for their forever homes, and I'm even more sold.

It's my destiny to work here. A college education will be great, no doubt. But if I could work here and get on the cheer squad, well…I'd truly be living my best life.

The line is moving relatively fast. I see a blonde woman about my age with curls and a rosy smile. My heart lifts. She looks like she'll be the one to talk to. I bet she'll be nice to me, whatever happens.

Just as she's serving the man in front of me, the door behind the counter swings open. I catch a glimpse of what's beyond, and it looks like a sort of anti-chamber between here and out the back. Perhaps a kitchen? Or some sort of prep room? That's probably to keep the cats away from the food, which also reassures me about the legitimacy of this concept. I'm all for kitty cuddles, but hygiene standards are important too.

I'm so busy musing on how the business actually operates that it takes me a second to absorb who it was that came through the door just now.

Oh.

I swallow as my widening eyes cast over the big guy carrying a tray of pastries that he swaps for the empty one that's sitting on the other side of the glass from me. His dark hair is closely shaved but he has a neatly trimmed beard that frames his face well. Tattoos cover his tanned forearms, and his white Toe Beans T-shirt clings to his solid frame like it's been sprayed on.

I guess I'm really not all that heartbroken with the full body shiver I have to repress. This guy is older and bigger than Parker, and I would much, *much* rather find myself under him any day of the week.

Focus! I tell myself. I'm not looking for a boyfriend. I'm looking for a job. Men can all go to hell for the foreseeable future as far as I'm concerned.

Which is a good thing because when Mr. Toe Beans straightens up with the empty tray, I find myself accidentally locking eyes with him.

And he's scowling.

He glances to see that the line is actually out the door now, so he looks back at me with a grunt and a nod of his head. I assume he's asking me what I'd like to order.

"Um, hi!" I say, giving him a little wave and then immediately regretting it. "I, uh, don't need anything. To buy, I mean. I guess I was wondering if you're hiring."

The guy—Nim, his badge reads. Interesting name. Anyway, Nim stares at me for a second. "No?" he says slowly, putting a whole lot of confusion into a one-syllable word.

I try my best not to get flustered. "I know you don't have any signs up or anything, I was just wondering. You see, I really need a job, and I really love cats. See!" I point to my headphones. "We always had cats at home until...well, we haven't had one for a couple of years. But I'm great with them! I think I'd be a perfect fit for this place and well, um, is there a manager or someone I could speak to?"

"I'm the manager," Nim says simply, still looking confused, his thick eyebrows knitted together.

"Oh," I utter, the first hint of defeat creeping in. "Right. So...are you sure? No vacancies at all? I'll do anything, really. I..."

I was trailing off anyway, but the words die in my throat as a tiny tabby kitten suddenly appears from nowhere, climbing up Mr. Manager like a tree until they reach his shoulder and perch there like they're the ruler of this small kingdom. Nim doesn't react at all, as if being used as a feline jungle gym is just part of his everyday life. It probably is. But his gruff, intimidating demeanor doesn't exactly match up with such a breathtakingly cute sight.

A sort of croaky sound escapes my throat as I try and process what I'm seeing while remembering what I was saying. I'm soon jolted back to reality, though.

"Come on, kid," the man behind me snaps. "He said no vacancies. Some of us need to get back to work."

I blink as I look down the line at more than one irritable face, then back at the manager who's still regarding me like an alien from outer space. All I did was ask if there were any jobs available, for crying out loud.

Of course there aren't, though. Why I thought the universe would be kind to me, I have no idea. Just because I would *love* a position here doesn't mean it's going to happen. That's not how life works.

"S-sorry," I mumble as I back away.

More people are watching me now. I sense it. Tears fill my eyes, and when I accidentally reverse into a table, they spill down my face. I spin around to check I haven't knocked anything over, the couple seated there looking up at me in alarm.

"Sorry!" I squeak at them before spinning again to face Nim once more. "Sorry to waste your time." I turn and flee, hating the happy sound of the bell as I practically pull the door off its hinges in my attempt to escape.

I run until I find a bench. It's covered in graffiti but other-wise looks clean. I slump down onto it, dropping my face into my hands as I cry. I might have worked out that Parker isn't the man I thought he was and that I don't actually want to be with him. But that doesn't stop the sharp pain of multiple rejections slicing through me.

Why would I think I could walk in there and get a dream job? I miss having a fur baby so much, but when our last cat crossed the rainbow bridge, with Mom's ongoing treatment, it didn't seem responsible to adopt anyone new.

I look back at the café and think about all those little kitties waiting for their forever homes.

Just like me, I guess.

That's stupid. I just need a place to rent for a while. Maybe when I was feeling particularly sad and lonely, I'd daydream that Parker was my forever, but I see now that was all it was—a dream.

I need a job and an apartment before I start classes in a week. But before that, I give myself a little bit of time to sit on this bench and have a good cry.

It's not like anyone's going to notice me or care, are they?

CHAPTER 4

Nim

I'M STILL STARING OUT THE DOOR, MY HEART IN MY THROAT, when I hear a dramatic sigh from my left.

I turn to see Leah glaring at me. It's such an unusual expression for her it makes me blink a couple of times. "What?"

"What do you mean—'what?'—Benjamin Decker?"

She only ever uses my actual name when I'm in real trouble. She's worked for me since the day I opened the café. If Donna is like my big sister, then Leah is my younger sibling. I don't even really think of her as an employee. That's why I let her get away with telling me off like that.

I'm just not sure exactly what I did wrong. My brain is still too busy short-circuiting.

That babbling young man with the kitten headphones was one of the most beautiful guys I've ever seen in my life. He had a tumble of dark curls, warm, sparkling eyes, and lips that looked so soft and kissable that I'd just wanted to brush my thumb over them.

He'd been talking about a job or something. But we weren't advertising anything.

And that's good because there's *no way* I want to be around that cutie in any kind of forced proximity. I'd never think straight again. And since it's me, no doubt I'd find a way to mess it up and hurt his feelings and...

Good lord, I'm acting like he'd even be interested in me. Just because I got cartoon cupids around my head doesn't mean a thing. He's probably not even a kitten in the lifestyle sense at all. Lots of people like those kinds of headphones. Why am I—

"Earth to Nim?"

I shake my head and look back at Leah. She's got her hands on her hips.

"Yeah?"

"Why were you mean to that poor boy?" she demands. "He looked crushed."

"We don't have any job vacancies," I reply, still feeling like my brain is doing a lot of catching up.

"Great!" some guy says in front of me. He's the one who yelled at the kitten. "Now we've established that for the fifth time, can I get an Americano and a bear claw to go?"

After the way he spoke to the kitten, I'm in no hurry to serve him. But I'm starting to realize, thanks to Leah, that the way *I* spoke to the kitten was not okay, either.

"Do you think I should go after him?"

Leah sighs and visibly softens. "That might be good for your karma, yeah." Then she plasters on her 'I'm smiling but fuck you' face and turns back to the customer. "One bear claw and one Americano coming right up, sir."

Before heading out, I grab my jacket and slip the little tabby from my shoulder inside. He knows not to jump out of his pocket, so he'll be safe to take with me like that. I've resisted naming him as he'll soon be big enough to go play in the café, and I'm sure someone will adopt him then. I'm very proud of the high turnaround numbers we have.

That's about all I'm feeling proud of right now. The daze is fading, and I'm seeing what an absolute ass I was to a kid who was just asking about getting work. He said he loved cats, right? He's probably a good person. He doesn't deserve to be treated like garbage because my body went into shutdown on account of how gorgeous he is. That's some creepy shit.

Urgh. This is why I try and avoid people like I do. I'm no good around them. Or for them.

It's suddenly very urgent that I catch up to him. He should have been long gone, but luck is on my side. He's about thirty feet away, sitting on the bench opposite the small, scruffy park.

His face is in his hands, but from the way his shoulders are shaking, I'm pretty sure he's crying.

Fuck.

It takes a lot to make me feel small, but I certainly shrink in on myself as I walk up to him, feeling incredibly sheepish.

"Hey," I say softly as I get close enough.

He jerks in surprise and looks up at me. I *hate* seeing his tear-streaked face. His lashes are spiky, and his eyes are red.

I did that. I'm a bastard.

"I—what? Sorry?" he stutters, looking around in his confusion.

"Can I sit?" I grunt.

He stares at me for a second before nodding. I perch myself on the edge, putting a couple of feet between us. The last thing I want to do is intimidate him further.

"I'm sorry," I say.

He frowns. "For what?"

"For being a dick."

He sniffs and takes a deep breath, sitting up a bit straighter. "You weren't, though. You don't have any jobs open, that's all you said. I went barging in there all excited and didn't listen to you."

It's my turn to frown. "I could have been nicer about it."

He looks me over. "Um, I guess. Thank you. But that's not why I'm upset. Not really. You didn't have to come out here. I saw how busy you are."

I shrug. "S'okay." I had to make sure he was all right, but that feels a bit much to tell him in the moment.

Really, I *should* go back to work. I know Leah isn't on her own, but I'm the boss. I never leave them in the lurch. However, I can't seem to get up and abandon this little kitten, not when he's looking so lost.

"Why, then?"

He blinks those pretty eyelashes at me. They're so long. "Why what?"

"Why are you crying?" I clarify.

"Oh," he says softly, wiping his hand across his face. "Uh… my life kind of went to shit in twenty-four hours and my head is still spinning." He laughs, but I get the feeling that it's not all that funny. "I thought a dream job in your amazing café would fix everything, but that's not how life works."

I lick my lips. "You think the café's amazing?" I ask quietly. I'm not an idiot. I know very well how popular the joint is. But hearing this sweet boy say so warms my cold, dead heart.

"Oh, yeah," he says with such enthusiasm. His face is still damp, but his eyes are suddenly sparkling. My poor heart is defenseless against it. "It's so cozy and I saw how well you're looking after the cats. I know you said you're the manager, but like, did you decorate it all and stuff yourself?"

"Yeah," I said, feeling a smile twitch at the corner of my mouth. People always think it's so weird that a guy like me would pick out doilies, but I just chose everything I thought my nana would like, and that seemed to be the right answer.

The kitten nods thoughtfully. "You should be proud."

We sit awkwardly for a minute as I scramble around for something to say. All I know is that I want to know more. I want to know *everything*. Even if the logical part of my brain is telling me that this kid doesn't need my grumpy ass in his life.

"So…you need a job?" I find myself asking instead.

He nods and sighs. "Yeah. As fast as I can, if possible. I need to find an apartment, too. Sorry, you don't care about all that." He laughs ruefully. "Like I said, this has all happened really fast, and I'm definitely still trying to wrap my head around it."

Oh, no. All my Daddy instincts are kicking off like someone just blasted a siren. For a moment, I struggle to find words, any words.

"What happened to your old apartment?" I manage eventually.

He pulls at his fingers and tries to smile, but it doesn't reach his eyes. "There wasn't one, it turns out. Long story short, I'm new in town because I'm supposed to be starting college, but my boyfriend broke up with me so now I'm sleeping in my car and I don't know what to do because apparently he was never my boyfriend this whole time. We were just fucking every once in a while, and I just imagined the whole loving boyfriend part. So…" He finally stops and takes a long breath, giving me a chance to process all that word vomit. "Sorry, that wasn't really the short version at all. Oh, and he was cheating on me. Or I guess he was cheating on that guy with me. I'm not entirely sure."

I grit my teeth and resist the urge to break something. I hate always being right. But the world is full of selfish pricks who just take what they want and trample on nice people as they do so.

He shakes his head and hugs himself. "Wow, I'm sorry.

You're a total stranger. You don't need my problems. Look, it's fine. There are plenty of more places to look for a job and—"

"What's your name?"

He blinks at me. "Huh?"

"What's your name?" I ask again. "I'm Nim."

"I know. It's on your badge," he says, jutting his chin at my chest. My jacket is actually covering it right now, so he must have noticed back at the café. "Uh, I'm Jessie. Jessie Garras. Nice to meet you, Nim."

I stick out my hand, waiting patiently until he gingerly shakes it.

"There we go," I grunt. "Not strangers anymore."

I release him, and he lets out a startled laugh. "Oh, okay, then," he says with a shy smile that melts my heart. "It's nice not to be completely alone in this town. Thank you for listening."

I open and close my mouth a couple of times. I don't want to overstep or interfere, but this boy doesn't have anyone looking out for him. In fact, it feels like the opposite.

"So you don't wanna go home?" I prompt. Maybe he *can't* go home.

He drops his head and swings his feet. "I'd rather not. Not because it's bad! I love my mom. It's back in Cincinnati. I've waited five whole years to go to college. If I can just get on my feet, I'd love to give Paddle Creek a real shot. My ex shouldn't get to ruin my life like that."

Part of me is relieved. Not that anything's going to happen, but I didn't think he looked eighteen. I'm much happier talking to a twenty-three-year-old. Also, that he's not afraid to go home. He'd just rather not give up on here just yet.

"Are you staying at the motel?" I ask. He's going to tell me to fuck off with all these questions soon, I'm sure. I would.

But actually...he sort of puffs up. Like he's not used to anyone paying attention to him.

God, it's like catnip to me.

"Uh, no. Not exactly," he says with a nervous laugh. "It's fine, though. I'll be fine. I've got a few days to get my shit together. I'm sure it'll work out. Thank you for coming out to find me, but I've already caused you enough trouble. You probably need to get back to work."

Rather than sounding like he's trying to get rid of me, he sounds deflated. Like he knows this—whatever is going on here—can't last.

But I'm not satisfied. Not until I know he's going to be okay if I walk away.

"So, where are you staying?" I push.

He shrugs and nibbles on his thumbnail. "I only got into town yesterday." I don't say anything. I just keep my gaze on him until he starts to squirm. I might not be *his* Daddy, but that doesn't mean I'm not above using Daddy tactics on him. Eventually, he cracks with a dismissive wave of his hand. "I slept in my car last night, but hopefully—"

"The *fuck?*" I blurt out so loudly I feel the little tabby in my pocket stir. Jessie also gapes at me. "Some shithead cheated on you, dumped you, and has left you to sleep in your fucking car. Have I got that right?"

Jessie shrinks back from me, which is the last thing I wanted him to do. But I'm also aware that I'm radiating fury, and don't blame him for wanting a bit more distance between the two of us.

"Honestly, it's not your problem," he says with a shaky smile, not sounding convinced at all. "I'm sorry I made a scene at your café, but—"

"Stop saying you're sorry," I grumble as I get to my feet and shove my hand at him again. This time it's not to shake but to pull him up as well. "You haven't done anything wrong, Jessie. Come on."

"Come…where?" he says uncertainly as he rises.

"You tell me," I reply. "Where's your car?"

He rubs the back of his neck. "Uh, I parked it in a lot a few blocks over. Why?"

"We need to get your stuff," I say, already marching in the direction he indicated.

"Oh-kay," he says, falling into step with me. "But *why*? I haven't got anywhere to go yet."

"Yes, you do," I say mulishly. "You're moving in with me."

CHAPTER 5

Jessie

What is happening right now?

No, I'm serious. Anyone know?

I traipse after Nim in a sort of daze, feeling like I don't have a choice. But I kind of *like* that. Wasn't this what Parker was supposed to do? Just…take care of me. I realize he never at any point agreed to that, and in the glaring light of day, I don't think he'd actually ever be capable of it. But whether or not I realized it, I think that's what I've been craving.

And somehow…it's just fallen right into my lap.

No. *No!* This guy is simply being nice. He feels sorry for me. I'm not sure what he really means about living with him or whatever. But if he's got a spare room that's safe and doesn't cost a fortune, good lord I'll jump at the chance.

"Um, here we go," I say sheepishly as we approach my car.

I'm confused as to why I'm bothering to be embarrassed now. He already knows my whole sorry state of affairs. I just wish it hadn't come to this. I spent so long looking after Mom and myself I thought moving to a new town would be a piece of cake. Instead, everything fell apart the moment I arrived.

My car is a hunk of junk, but she's got me this far in life, and I can't help but love her. The silver body has some dents, and I dread to think how many miles she has on the clock, but she's never not started on me yet. Her name is Purrse-phone. Not that anyone but my mom knows that.

I walk toward the trunk to get whatever of my stuff we can carry. But Nim goes to the passenger side door, tries the locked handle, then looks expectantly at me.

"Oh, um," I utter. "Are you...? Did you want to...uh?"

"We're driving back to the café," he says like it was obvious.

I look at him for a second. He's not mad at me, but he does have an expectant look on his face. I'm not sure what's going on, but I don't really feel like I'm in the position to be questioning anything, either. If he says he's going to help me, I have this crazy notion that's exactly what he intends to do.

"Uh, right. Okay, then."

I jog around to the driver's side and unlock the car so we can both get in. He immediately pushes his seat back so his knees aren't shoved up against the dash. Why is that so hot? Parker was a bit taller and bulkier than me, but I never found it a turn-on. Probably best to just ignore how I'm feeling.

"Sorry," I mumble at the teeny size of my car. He shrugs and reaches for his seatbelt, so I follow suit.

Naturally, I have an air freshener in the shape of a paw and a stuffie purple kitty sitting on the dash. Out of the corner of my eye I see him take in both, but of course he doesn't say anything. Well, he knows I'm cat crazy, just like he knows I slept in here last night. He's fully aware of what he's getting himself into.

I'm able to drive us back toward the café without the need for directions, but as we get closer, I'm not sure what I'm supposed to do. There's a little on-street parking, but not much. He points and juts his chin.

"Left."

I see a small side alley, so I signal and take us down there. We end up behind the stores with the dumpsters—but also a handful of parking spaces, some of which are empty.

"There," he says as he jabs his finger at one of the vacant ones.

"Oh...it doesn't belong to anyone?" I check even though I'm already pulling in.

"Yeah, me," he grunts.

"Oh, right. And, um, you don't need it for your own car?"

I glance over just in time to witness the barest hint of a smile twitch at his lips. "No. That's mine."

I look back at where he's pointing this time, and my eyebrows rise as I bring the car to a stop and pull the parking brake up. Against the building, tucked in between the dumpster and the back of Toe Beans, is an enormous black motorcycle that makes my heart race just looking at it.

"You ride that?" I splutter.

This time, he gives me an actual smile, even if his lips are still pressed together. "Yeah," he says softly. "Come on."

He leaves me sitting in the car for a moment, my jaw hanging slightly open as I look at the Harley-Davidson for another few seconds. I'm equally terrified and enthralled by it. What must it feel like speeding along the open road on that thing?

When I realize he's opened up the trunk, I leap out of the car and rush over to him. "Oh, you don't have to..." I protest weakly, but he's already gotten out my suitcase and a number of bags and boxes. I thought I packed pretty light, all things considered. But looking at all my stuff now and thinking about it in a stranger's space, I feel it's a huge amount.

Hang on a minute. Where *is* he planning to take it all?

"Huh. Are you...giving me a cat bed?" I joke. But seriously

—if I have to sleep in the café, I will. It'll be safer and more horizontal than Purrsephone, that's for sure.

He grunts again, but this time it sounds a little bit more like a laugh. "I live up there." He points above the café, and my eyebrows rise once more.

"No way," I say as I exhale. "That's so cool."

He gives me that same sideways glance he did when I said that Toe Beans was awesome. I hope he doesn't think I'm being sarcastic, because I'm really not. The idea of living above your job is awesome because in theory, you'd never be late.

But more importantly, that means he's right next to the cats that live in the café. That warms me from the inside. Those kitties have got to live an odd life with people coming and going all the time. It feels like the café—specifically, Nim —really does have their best interests at heart.

He looks between us and all my stuff. "I think we're gonna need two trips," he says.

"I'm so sorry—" I begin.

"Stop that," he says firmly, frowning at me. I gulp and repress a full-body shiver. Why is that *also* hot? "I volunteered to help. There's nothing to apologize for."

"Um, okay," I say softly. "Thank you."

He hums and grabs a stack of boxes in one arm and my suitcase in another. My eyes feel like they're bugging out of my head as I watch him walk toward the building, thinking about how much that all weighs. Then I come back to my senses and pick up a few things myself before closing the trunk and hurrying after him.

In an impressive move, he manages to get his keys out of his pocket and open the door all while still juggling my crap. I follow him up the stairs to the next story, where again, he singlehandedly lets us into his apartment.

I'm sure there is furniture and doors and windows and stuff. That's kind of the definition of an apartment, right?

All I see is cats. Black cats.

We step directly into the living room, and Nim sticks his feet out left then right to stop any of the kitties from darting outside. I follow his lead and dash quickly inside so I can close the door behind me. But as soon as I can, I find a space to put down what I'm carrying and drop to my knees, reaching out and offering the backs of my hands to the cats.

"Hi!" I squeak as the bold ones come up to sniff me. Some rush into other rooms to hide, and some watch me from afar. "Hey, there. How are you doing? I'm Jessie. Nice to meet you."

I'm so enraptured as at least half a dozen babies circle around me, it takes me a second to realize that Nim is staring at me. I open my mouth to apologize, but he's told me off for that. So I snap it shut and look over all the cats before glancing at him again.

"I'll put these in your room," is all he says before spinning around and heading through the archway and up the stairs I can just about see from where I am. Wow. His apartment has two levels? I guess I feel a little less guilty about crashing here.

Soon, I've got one cat in my lap and another perched on my shoulders. Several more are rubbing against me, swishing their tails. A chorus of purring surrounds me, and I hardly notice as Nim creeps back down to pick up the bags and boxes I unceremoniously dropped when I realized there were cats I could be meeting instead.

When he comes back, he stands awkwardly for a second until I spy him lurking. "Is everything okay?" I ask, immediately worrying that I've been lazy in playing with the kitties instead of carrying stuff.

He shakes his head. "I mean, yes," he contradicts himself. "I just need your keys to get the rest."

I look down at all the cats climbing onto me. "Oh, yeah, I should—"

He shakes his head again. "I've got it. They like you."

He doesn't exactly smile. However, there's something warm in the way he's looking at me that means I don't argue. I just hand over Purrsephone's keys.

It's wild that I was crying on a park bench half an hour ago. And now I've got a small black and fluffy army headbutting me that all together sounds like a lawn mower. I notice that they have different colored collars on, each with a silver disk. I think they're named after zodiac signs, which is cute. Even for the most dedicated pet owner, that would be the only way to tell each of these adorable voids apart. Every one of them is as dark as night.

The door rattles and I jump, scaring away a few of my new friends. But obviously, it's just Nim with my last few bits. He pauses at the threshold and looks at me looking at him.

"Everything all right?" he asks.

I laugh and rub the back of my neck. "Yeah, of course," I say. "I've just been making friends. This is like a dream. They're all so cute."

I bite my lip to stop myself from talking. He doesn't seem to notice. Instead, he nods and pushes all the way into the room, letting the door swing shut behind him. He makes it halfway across the room before I break.

"Why are they all black?" I blurt out.

He freezes. Then he turns just his head, peeking at me over his shoulder. The arched eyebrow is the only indication I get that I should continue speaking.

"The cats," I manage to elaborate. "Why are they all the same?"

His shoulders sag, and he drops his head. For a moment, I think he's not going to reply.

When he does, I can barely make out all the words as he mumbles them together.

"Nooneeverwantstheblackcats."

"Uh?" I say before I can think.

He clears his throat. "No one *ever* wants the black cats," he says quietly. I look around, my heart sinking. Before I can question him, he speaks again. "People think if rescue cats have one eye, a mangled ear, or are missing a leg, they'll get left behind. But those go so fast. People are kind like that. Black cats are ordinary. They're bad luck. They get left behind."

That's easily the most words he's strung together so far. I find it hard to swallow, and my eyes sting. "Oh," I say softly. "So…you…"

"They don't have to keep wondering if they'll get a forever home now," he says gruffly. He clears his throat more forcefully and shrugs my boxes in his arms. My kitty backpack is slung over his broad shoulder. It looks comically small. "I'll get these to your room."

I watch silently as he stomps out of sight. Meanwhile, I feel like my heart has been shredded.

He keeps the cats that no one else will take. How heartbreakingly beautiful is that?

Looking around at where I've found myself, I suddenly wonder if I'm actually in *more* trouble, not less.

Nim might be scary. And he's definitely still a stranger. But he's also someone who rescues stray cats when they have nowhere else to go. Including the human kind of kitty.

I might have promised to swear off men for the foreseeable future. But I'd have to have a heart of stone to ignore how utterly compassionate that is. Kindness is a rare attribute these days, sadly. I find it very attractive.

That's on top of the man himself with his muscles and tattoos and sparkling hazel eyes.

And now we're going to be living together. I have literally no idea for how long.

How am I going to stop myself from falling head over heels for this guy?

CHAPTER 6

Nim

Apparently, I have completely lost my mind.

The reason we're in this mess is because my brain blue-screened and, in an effort to stay away from this precious kitten, I told him the cold hard fact that we weren't hiring. Thanks to my ogre-like behavior, said kitten is now *living with me*.

There is no possible way this won't end in disaster.

As I set the last of his things down in my spare room, I take a second to breathe deeply, trying to get some much-needed oxygen to my brain. I also pinch my nose for good measure, hoping some kind of clarity is going to come to me.

The only thing I understand right now is how fucked I am.

If I think properly on it, though, it's fine. It might be hell for me, but I am never, ever going to cross any lines with him. He'd never be interested in me like that anyway, I'm sure. He's just had his heart broken by a douchebag, and when he's ready to start dating again, it'll be with someone he meets at college or something. Someone who'll be his own age—that's my point. Most people don't like a big age gap.

Most people don't want to be Daddied. Certainly not the way I do it, apparently.

Brent's parting remarks still sting, even after three years. You don't get called a patronizing, emotionally stunted robot and forget it in a hurry. He wasn't wrong, I guess. I'm no good with people, let alone as a boyfriend. Words don't come naturally to me. I thought he wanted me to take care of him, but it seems I just ended up smothering him.

Paddle Creek was supposed to be a fresh start. For the most part, it has been. I needed to get away from the home I built with Brent and back to the people I called family. I had to give to the community again, even if I can only bear to skirt on the edges myself. Because otherwise, when my time comes, I don't want to reminisce on my life and wonder if I ever even lived it.

I take another breath. So that's all I'm doing with Jessie. I'm paying a kindness forward that I never had when I was first out on my ass and all alone.

Being kicked out by your family after they realize you're gay is such a cliché, but it's heartbreaking how much it still happens, even today. Back in the late nineties, it was pretty common. My dad didn't think twice about chasing me from the house with a baseball bat. My mom at least grabbed me some clothes and all the cash she had in her purse, but I still never saw or heard from her again.

I know my nana would have taken me in, but she passed the year before. My memories of her still shine brightly, though. That's why when I opened my own business, I poured so much of her into it. She always had a soft spot for the neighborhood cats, too.

Life was *rough* for a while. I went into foster care for a bit and bounced around shelters. I dropped out of school so I could work a couple of menial jobs, but I spent more than my fair share of nights sleeping on the streets. I'm perfectly well aware that's why I love cats so much. During that time, they were the only creatures who showed me any real affection. They certainly didn't judge me.

Eventually, I saved up enough for a crappy room to call my own and, more importantly, my first bike. It was only an old Suzuki, but it gave me the kind of freedom I'd never had in my life. When I was introduced to the Cardinals in Indianapolis, they probably never really understood how they brought me back from the brink.

They gave me stability and purpose, enough that I was able to go to night school and get not only my GED but also complete a course in business and accounting. They pointed me in the direction of Paddle Creek when Brent left and I needed a fresh start. Without them, I never could have opened Toe Beans.

More than that, though, they gave me a family and a community. Which is why the sheriff coming and asking questions at O'Toole's irked me so much. Nobody messes with my family, not now I'm big enough to fight back. I just hope that nuisance call was a one-time thing.

That's all to say if I can pay even a fraction of my debt to them forward with Jessie, then my karma that Leah is always warning me about will be even. That's why I'm going out of my way to help him like this.

No other reason.

He doesn't have much stuff, but it'll be nice to see this room being used for once. I've offered it to people, but as everyone I know lives locally, there's never been a need for it. Until now.

I wonder how long he'll want to stay—or need to. On the drive over, he mentioned that he's applied for accommodation at the college, but there's a waiting list. I can't help but think that's a waste of money, though. He said it had taken him until now to even get to college. The way he talked about his mom I sense there's a story lurking not too far beneath the surface.

I've always had a keen eye for those in need of a little TLC. Speaking of which, I check in on the sleeping kitten still in my pocket. He wasn't bothered by all the moving of boxes or traveling in the car. Wherever he ends up calling home, I know he's going to be bombproof.

But that little kitten in my living room? I'm not so sure. The way his shoulders were shaking on that park bench broke my heart. He's one bit of bad luck away from his ninth life, and I'll be damned if I'm the reason that happens.

Even if I can't be his Daddy, I can be strong for him. I can ease his burdens and keep him safe. That's what Daddying is all about. I don't need the physical side of things.

Well, I'd like that, but I can't have it. So there's no sense in stressing over it.

I also can't hide up here forever, so with a sigh, I head back downstairs. I'm way, seriously overdue back in the café anyway. So I need to make sure Jessie is settled, then run back down there. First, we need to talk through a few things, though.

But all thoughts fall out of my head as I walk back into the living room and see that he's still sitting on the floor, surrounded by most of my pride of wayward cats. He's calmly stroking them and letting them sniff him and climb all over him. He's smiling and murmuring softly to them, his brown eyes sparkling with excitement.

He wasn't kidding. He really does love cats.

It's impossible to stop my heart from melting at the sight. If I were any kind of photographer or artist, I'm sure I'd be itching to capture the moment. As it is, I just stare for as long as possible, hungrily committing the image to my mind.

Eventually, he notices me and grins in my direction. "I can't believe you're really going to let me stay with all these amazing fur babies," he says. I don't miss how his voice catches with emotion. "Thank you, Nim. This is like a dream."

I shrug and shove my hands into my pockets. "S'okay," I say. "Stay as long as you need."

He bites his lip and looks down at the kitty he's currently petting. They're wearing a purple collar, so it's got to be Leo.

"I don't want to be an imposition," he says, sounding unsure.

"You're not," I tell him honestly. No one else is using that room, are they?

He nods, but he still looks worried. "How much rent do you want to charge? It might take me a minute to start paying, but once I get a job, I can—"

I manage to cut him off by shaking my hands and taking a step closer. "No rent. Don't worry."

He blinks at me. "I can't just live here for free."

I shrug again. "You'll probably need to buy your share of groceries," I admit. I want to take care of him, but I do have to be realistic.

He blinks at me. "Of course I will, but…" He casts his gaze around before his eyes light up. "How about until I get a job, I can take care of the kitties? I bet just feeding them and cleaning out their litter boxes takes a fair bit of time."

I won't lie, I almost whimper at the thought of an extra hour in bed each morning. I would never, ever neglect my cats. But he's right. Having ten of them takes up a lot of time when my day starts so early as it is.

"Sure," I grunt. "And if you don't mind doing that…well, you could help out in the café too. I can pay you minimum wage."

His eyes widen. It's amazing how much that makes me want to squirm. *I'm* supposed to be the Daddy here, for crying out loud.

"I thought you weren't hiring," he says slowly.

"We're not," I say honestly. "But I can squeeze in a few hours' pay from the budget if that's what you want. But *no* paying rent. Save it up for a deposit when you move."

His mouth is hanging open, but it soon stretches into a wide grin. Carefully, he detangles himself from my cats, then he dashes over to me. I'm not prepared for the way he throws his arms around my neck, standing on his tiptoes and squealing. *Fuck.* He feels so good. He *smells* so good despite sleeping in his car the night before.

"Thank you, thank you, *thank you!*" he cries, giving me an extra tight squeeze before letting me go. He dances on the spot, wiggling his fingers, probably completely oblivious as to how fast my heart is racing. "I will be the best cat servant you've ever seen, I promise! Just tell me what to do."

He licks his lips and looks so earnestly at me my brain is dangerously close to blinking out on me again. "Uhh... they're good for now. I need to get back to the café. How about a tour? You can, uh, shower and get comfortable until I get back."

"Sure," he says with a nod and a smile. "Well, I've already seen the living room, so that's a good start. I enjoy that there's only one sofa and five cat trees. Seems like a sensible ratio."

He pokes out his tongue and sways from side to side. I'm not always sure if he's joking when he says things like that. My old man wielded sarcasm with excruciating consequences. But when Jessie teases, it feels warm. Considering how broken and apologetic he was when we met, it's quite remarkable that this cheeky side is still so strong. He's challenging without being annoying or mean. He'd make someone a beautiful boy or kitten, I'm sure.

Not me, though.

I clear my throat and try not to think about what will

happen if we both want to watch TV and there's only one sofa. Hopefully, he'll want to watch his own sort of stuff on his laptop or something. We can cross that bridge if and when we come to it.

"The kitchen's through here," I say, turning and walking through the archway. "Most of the cats know to stay off the counter. I've got anti-bacterial wipes in the cupboard here if you need them, but I don't ever spray the cats with water or anything to keep them down."

I'm very firm about that. If he's got a problem with that rule, he'll be looking for a new apartment sooner rather than later.

He's frowning at me. "Of course not," he says, reaching out to stroke Taurus, who has—on cue—jumped up to swish her tail in our faces. "This is their home as much as ours. I'll just work around them."

I let out the breath I wasn't aware I'd been holding. It's not like I meant to set him a sneaky test or anything, but it still feels good that he passed.

With a nod, I move back into the hall. He can work out where the fridge is, I'm sure, and both the oven and microwave are pretty self-explanatory.

"Bathroom," I say, pointing at it as we pass. The door is open, so he can see there's a shower above the tub and a reasonable amount of space. "Spare towels," I add as we go past the linen cupboard. "My room."

Thankfully, the door is closed. It's intimate enough having him sharing my space, but at least in there, I'll be able to hide from him.

My thoughts will be harder to escape, I have no doubt.

I realize that's the full extent of the downstairs tour, so I turn around again to face him, finding him right in front of me, smiling excitedly.

"I love it!" he chirps. "So, I'm upstairs?"

Silently, I nod, making my way toward the stairs and trusting he'll follow. Of course he does.

Technically, this is the bigger bedroom. I could have taken it for myself, but I preferred to live all on the same level. So while this room does have a bed, it also has a lot of crap piled up along the side, including several boxes of clothes and old DVDs, empty suitcases, a treadmill I never use (but certainly hang laundry on), and two more cat trees.

"Sorry," I say, indicating the mess with my hand.

He snorts at me. "Now who's apologizing? You've given me a free room. I can deal with a few boxes. Nim, seriously. This is amazing. I can't believe it. I'm going to sleep like an absolute log tonight."

He laughs, and I notice a little dimple on his right cheek for the first time. I want to nuzzle my nose against it. That, combined with the knowledge that we'll be sleeping under the same roof later has me almost breaking out in a cold sweat.

"Okay, well, yeah," I say, scratching the back of my neck. "I'll be back around five-ish probably. Have a shower, unpack…whatever you need. Uh, yeah…"

In my haste to leave, I back into the doorframe. He waves at me before I jog down the stairs.

This is going to be absolute hell.

What was I thinking?

CHAPTER 7

Jessie

I KNOW PEOPLE TALK ABOUT GOING INTO SHOCK IN A MEDICAL way. I don't know if that's what's happening to me, but my brain kind of whited out as soon as Nim left me by myself.

Well, I'm far from alone. I'm reminded of this fact as several sets of paws stomp over me where I'm lying on my new bed, staring at the ceiling as my mind slowly attempts to process all the many thoughts whirring around my head.

There's a strong chance that Nim isn't a serial killer. I think I'm okay staying here. He's got nice vibes. Quiet, but nice. But he's also seriously hot, and his offer to let me live here rent-free is definitely too good to be true, right? What's the catch?

Well, I suppose agreeing to feed and clean up after almost a dozen cats will go a fair way to earning my keep. I think I counted ten, but I have to double-check. He's still going to pay me a little to help out in the café as well, so I still feel like I'm kind of ripping him off.

Maybe once I start classes, a room might become available in the dorms, or with the cheerleading house if there is one. In that case, I won't have to worry about being a burden for too long.

In the meantime, I decide that I can make myself feel less weird and awkward by being super helpful. The realization galvanizes me, and I sit up, blinking, only disturbing a couple of kitties.

"I am going to be the best houseguest ever!" I declare to them.

But first, a shower.

I haven't washed up since I left home early yesterday morning. After the drive, the crying, the restless night, the walking from store to store, and the carrying of my belongings up and down various stairs, I am so ready for a change of clothes and a good rinse. I'm tempted to run a bath, but that feels a little too extravagant, not to mention there's a real danger that I'll fall asleep in there if I do.

Instead, I grab my things from my suitcase and hurry down to the bathroom, leaving the door open so my new feline friends can come and go as they please. It's so funny how cats act like a closed door is the end of the world sometimes.

It's not long before I'm naked and hopping into the tub. There's a curtain that I pull all the way across for some privacy, then I get the water running as hot as I can stand. *Urgh,* it's glorious. I can practically feel all my stress melting away as I let the stream pound against my sore muscles.

Not wanting to use up too much water, I wash my hair and body as fast as possible, but then...oh dear. Being completely alone is a novelty for me after living with my mom all these years. I don't know how long I'll be living here or if I'll have to share a bathroom in my next place. Chances are high.

Fuck it. To say I've been stressed and depressed is an

understatement. I deserve a little release, and it's not like it's going to hurt anyone.

I close my eyes and wrap my hand around my hardening length. I still don't want to waste too much water, but I have a feeling this won't take long.

Moaning, I start to stroke my hardening dick. Try as I might, thoughts of a certain burly, tattooed biker with a soft spot for stray kitties drift into my mind. I know I shouldn't be abusing thoughts of Nim like this, but I can't stop myself from imagining that he's slipped into the shower with me, coming up from behind and taking me in hand himself. He'd be so much bigger than me, his hairy chest pressed against my back as he kisses my neck…

I bite my lip and tug at one of my nipple piercings. God, I bet he's the *best* at spooning. I'd feel so safe snuggled up against him. Especially if he put his big hands on me and whispered naughty things in my ear. I bet he makes up for all the not-talking during the day by being an absolute beast in the bedroom. *Urgh.* I'd be so good for him, I'd do anything he wanted, I-I-I…

My orgasm hits me hard, and I explode all over the tiles with a guttural cry. Panting and shivering, I blink my eyes open, watching as the water washes away all the evidence of my very wrong thinking from my hand, belly, and the wall.

After a minute or so, my heart rate and breathing start to return to normal. Guilt threatens to creep in, but I shake my head. "I didn't do anything wrong," I say out loud, shutting off the water. "No one ever needs to know."

I'm soon distracted as I pull back the curtain and realize that I forgot to pick myself up a towel. Shit. Okay, I'll use the one that's on the rack and then put a fresh one out for Nim. If I can work out how to use the washing machine, I can even clean this one for him.

Besides, I kind of like using his towel, knowing that it's

been on his skin as well. It's probably naughty, but after that incredible orgasm, I'm not feeling very saintly in this moment.

A little while later, I am clean and dry in a pair of cloth booty shorts and a crop top that reads 'I licked it, so it's mine.' I figured I'll get hot and sweaty with all the unpacking and stuff, and having just had a shower, that seemed like a waste. So I picked a skimpy outfit to run around the apartment with, planning on giving myself time to change into something less provocative before Nim comes back.

I hate having cold feet, though. So I've got both a pair of socks on as well as my fat slippers that look like paws. I also find one of my soft headbands with kitty ears on. With no one else around, I can put my music on out loud so there's no need for my headphones. But the idea of wearing my ears now is comforting for some reason.

It's probably weird, but sometimes I just like to pretend I *am* a cat. It delights me, and for some reason, it calms me down. Like when I'm Kitty Jessie, I don't have to worry about so many things.

Of course I've *never* admitted that out loud to anyone before. I thought about telling Parker several times, but I'm really glad I didn't now. I convinced myself that he'd understand and be supportive, but there was obviously a reason I never confided in him. After the way he treated me yesterday, I have a sinking feeling that he'd probably have been quite cruel about the whole thing.

Well, screw him. He's in the past now. And—not that I ever intend on contacting him again—I plan on thriving. But this town is small. We could very well accidentally run into each other. I want him to regret thinking I was something that he could just throw away without a second thought.

I use a tote to create a laundry bag, tossing my worn clothes in there along with thoughts of my ex. "Be gone!" I cry, willing it into the universe. "This is a new Parker-free zone!"

Putting on one of my peppy pop music playlists, I start dancing around the room as I unpack. Without even really thinking about it, I begin to tidy some of Nim's stuff as well. Hopefully, I'm not overstepping, but I get the feeling he doesn't bother with the things in here all that much. So why not make it neater while I'm at it?

In no time at all, the room is looking like *my* room. I don't have anything to put on the walls—that would be a step too far anyway—but I've got kitty stuffies on the bed and my rainbow lamp on the nightstand. My clothes might be hidden away in the drawers, and I've got other stuff stored under the bed, but those little touches make the room feel like mine.

I bite my lip as an unexpected wave of emotion hits me. For the first time since I left, I feel like calling my mom. The idea of telling her just how spectacularly things fucked up yesterday was too much to bear. But now I've landed on my feet—like a good cat should—I want to let her know I'm okay.

Hmmm…maybe not all the details right now. I'm still not sure how to explain what's going on with Nim, even to myself. So instead of calling, I take a photo of my cute room, strategically angling it so the least amount of boxes are in view. Then I message her, saying that things didn't work out with Parker but that it was for the best and I'm now with a different friend and everything's okay. I also take a selfie with the first black kitty that allows me to cuddle them to my chest, telling Mom that the place even has fur babies. Jackpot!

I don't let on how many fur babies exactly. She'd never believe me.

That done, I decide to start earning my keep, and go in hunt of the vacuum cleaner, finding it tucked away in the linen cupboard which also reminds me to get out a fresh towel for the bathroom. Once I've hung that up (and made sure my damp one is drying on my door), I attack the apartment with the vacuum, blasting my music even louder so I can hear it over the din.

It's interesting to see which cats run and which stick around to investigate what I'm doing. At the moment, they're just a bunch of different colored collars to me. But hopefully soon, I'll start remembering their names and personalities.

By the time I'm done cleaning, it's still only four o'clock. But I realize I haven't actually eaten today. I chew on my thumbnail and consider my options. I can't leave the apartment, because I don't have a key. I don't want to raid Nim's cupboards. He said many things, but he didn't actually say I could eat his food. However…what if I made us both dinner for when he got back? That would probably be okay, right?

First things first, I should probably check and see what he's got. If the fridge is empty, there won't be much I can do. To my surprise, it's nicely stocked, and so are the cupboards. There's a hairy moment when I almost find myself the victim of a cat food avalanche, but I manage to steady all the neatly stacked cans just in time.

My heart rate still slightly elevated after that excitement, I go back and look at everything with a more focused mind. What meal could I actually make? When I discover a pack of ground beef that's due to expire the following day, I decide on lasagna. My mouth waters at just the thought of it.

I plug my phone into charge as I realized it was running on fumes, then get to work making the two sauces that will go between the pasta sheets. Dancing around the kitchen to Taylor Swift and Ariana Grande, I sing my heart out, feeling down to my bones how fortunate my luck turned out.

A little sob escapes from somewhere, and I take a moment to rest my hand on my chest and blink away the tears. "Oh, it's okay, sweetheart," I say, soothing myself. "You're all right. Everything's going to be okay. I promise. You've got Nim now."

Honestly, I don't know what's going to happen with this man I only just met a couple of hours ago. But I truly believe I've made a friend. One who has nothing to do with Parker. I've got a place to sleep and a dream part-time job. Next week I'll start my classes and try out for the cheer squad. And on top of all that, the whole reason I'm here is because my mom beat cancer's ass.

What more can I really ask for than that?

A rather apt Kelly Clarkson song comes on, and I squeal, hastily returning to stir my sauces that I momentarily neglected. I sing along to the words about how I'm so much stronger now, feeling every single lyric in my heart. "Yes, girl!" I cry out loud. "You know it!"

Nim said he was going to come back around five o'clock. It's ten to now, so hopefully, my timing is bang on. I put the lasagna in the oven on a low heat to let it cook slowly. I wash the bigger items and load the rest into the dishwasher, making sure the kitchen is even more sparkling than when I started.

My kitty companions have all been very well behaved, I have to admit. They must know what cooking is and that the stove is dangerous, so they stayed a safe distance away. But once I drift back into the living room, I soon have a trail of followers like the pied piper, several of them meowing for my attention.

"Yes, yes, I'm here," I assure them through a yawn. Suddenly, I'm exhausted. I guess it's been a couple of crazy days. Nim is due home any minute, so it won't hurt if I maybe lie down on the sofa for a moment and close my eyes. There's even a blanket hanging over the back that I pull over me. Before I snuggle down, I turn off my music and set an alarm on my charged-up phone so the lasagna doesn't catch fire.

But then I'm ensconced on the couch with a number of kitties curling up around me, purring softly. I'm pretty sure this is some kind of heaven. Yeah, a little cat nap won't hurt, I'm sure…

CHAPTER 8
Nim

It would be awesome if I could take my mind off Jessie for two seconds or more. I try and focus on serving customers and replenishing stock, but my brain is stuck on a loop, thinking about the adorable human kitten I've stashed upstairs in my apartment. I told him to take a shower, for crying out loud. That means he's going to be *naked.*

Even if I wanted to forget about him, every now and then, I catch a snippet of loud singing coming through the ceiling and glance upward, assuming that has to be him. Nobody's ever been in my home while I've been at work before, except for the cats, so I had no idea if sound traveled or not.

Apparently, it does.

I cast my eyes down again and find Leah grinning at me. She's still making three coffees at once, but that isn't stopping her from doing whatever is going on with her face.

"What?" I grunt.

She holds her hands up. "Did I say anything?"

"Not with your mouth," I grumble, rearranging cookies.

We're getting close to the end of the day, so it's time to bundle what we have left all together in the hopes of selling it before we close. Whatever's still here after that gets boxed up and taken to the town's retirement home. They insist on paying me pennies for it, but I'd give it to them for free if I could. I abhor food waste, plus I know what it's like to feel like you've been forgotten about. Some of those residents never get any visitors. I like to think my goodies give them something to look forward to every day.

Leah has apparently served her coffees and is now back to grinning in front of me like a lunatic. As we're nearing closing, that also means our walk-in customers have dwindled to only one or two every few minutes. Sadly, that means I'm limited with things I can distract her with.

"So you went out to apologize to that adorable boy, and instead ended up bringing him *home* with you like he's one of these kittens here."

Automatically, I glance down to where the tabby spent most of his afternoon, but I'm not wearing my jacket anymore. I've put him back in his pen for the evening, so he can't protect me from Leah's infuriating insinuations.

"I'm just helping him out," I mumble, moving around her. I don't have an objective in mind other than to get away from her. But there's nowhere to go without leaving her to fend for herself at the counter, and I did that for long enough today already. Sighing, I turn back around, feeling defeated.

Sure enough, she's beaming with her hands on her hips. "Uh-huh. And the fact that he's an adorable, pretty kitty boy has nothing to do with it."

Damn it. I wish I'd never drunkenly confessed to her once that I was a kitten Daddy. She was never uncool about it, but it meant right now, she knew far more than I was comfortable with.

"No, it doesn't," I insist.

It's partly true. Yeah, his nature kicked off all my protective instincts. But like I promised myself earlier—nothing is ever going to happen. He's depending on me for his accommodation. I couldn't possibly put him in an uncomfortable position.

She opens her mouth, I imagine to argue some more, but a customer appears behind her.

"Excuse me?" a prim woman in her forties or fifties says. Her blonde hair is in an immaculate bun on top of her head, and her lips and long nails are all crimson.

"Hi, there," Leah says immediately, spinning around with her friendly face plastered on. "How can I help you?"

"I'd like to speak to your manager," the woman replies with a cool smile.

Give me strength, I think as I trudge forward. "Yep, hi," I say, not in the mood for any bullshit. We're supposed to close our doors at four and have everything sorted by five. The night staff will come in to clean and tend to the cats later in the evening, but I'm keen to leave on time today.

I've got someone waiting for me for the first time ever.

She's still got that smile on her red lips that doesn't meet her eyes as she waves her hand around. "Is all this really hygienic?"

I frown and cross my arms. "Yeah," I say, not sure what else to add.

Leah jumps in, of course. There's a reason she's supposed to be the one who does the heavy lifting with customer service. But people always want the damned manager.

"You can see all our certifications on the wall here, ma'am," she says brightly, waving her own hand. "We have strict procedures for keeping our kitties out of the food prep area. All baking actually happens off-site, and we basically just unwrap and display all our food. The coffee is freshly brewed, though. Can I interest you in one?"

Leah's smile never falters but I can tell she's irritated. I don't blame her. Who comes to a cat café if they've got hang-ups with cleanliness or whatever? This woman should take herself into Albertson. They have plenty of fancy tea rooms and restaurants and such.

Mrs. Crimson gives us a prim little "hmph" noise and a twitch of her glossy lips. "No thank you. I'm not convinced it won't have cat hair floating in it. Have a good day."

With that, she sniffs, casts her gaze over my beloved café, then swans out. Her heels click-clack on the tiled floor, and her skirt and blouse are so tight around her hourglass figure I'm surprised she's not squeaking.

There's a beat when Leah and I just stare after her as the door swings shut. Then Leah raises her hand. "Sure, come back soon!" she says cheerfully, before spinning around and mouthing *"What the fuck?"* at me.

I shrug. "Some people just like to pee in other people's cornflakes," I say with a sigh. I know everything is fine. If she doesn't want to eat here, that's her business. Plenty of other people do.

Leah rolls her eyes and mutters a few more choice curses under her breath, but then she sighs and looks at the clock on the wall. Naturally, it's got illustrated cats all over it. My nana would have loved it.

"Look, we're almost done here," Leah says fondly, walking over and patting my chest. "Why don't you head off and make sure that pretty boy hasn't flooded your bathroom or anything."

The way she glances at the ceiling tells me that she's caught some of Jessie's private concert as well. I can't help but let out a little snort of amusement.

"I can't—" I start to say. I left her and the team alone for most of the afternoon already.

But she shakes her head and cuts me off. "When do you ever—and I mean *ever*—take vacation days?" I mumble something about the café needing me. She cups her hand around her ear and smirks triumphantly. "Yeah, never. That's what I thought. So go on, skedaddle."

I narrow my eyes at her and chew my lip for a second. "I suppose if I leave now, I can get a set of keys cut for him before the store closes."

She smacks my arm. "Atta-boy! Off with you."

I grumble some more, but actually, I'm grateful. It's not like my mind was completely here anyway.

It's just because this all happened literally hours ago. I'm not going to be preoccupied thinking about him all the time. Everything is so new that I simply want to make sure he's okay.

Giving him his own keys so he's not trapped will go a long way toward that. So I get my shit together and march into town. There's no point taking the bike when the hardware store is only a couple of blocks away.

There's a bit of a line, but I don't mind waiting. This is a job that needs doing. There's already enough of a power imbalance between Jessie and me, so I don't want him to feel beholden to me. He should be free to come and go as he likes.

I use the time I'm waiting to mentally make a grocery list, thinking about what I can cook us for dinner when I get home. I have no idea if he has any allergies. I'll have to check. In the meantime, a veggie stir fry with rice seems a safe enough bet, so once I have the keys, I then make my way over to the grocery store. I've got plenty of stuff in the kitchen, I'm sure, but I feel like fresh vegetables is the right move for our first meal together.

It's been so long since I've had anyone over for dinner. I hope it's not going to be awkward. I don't even have a dining room table. We'll have to eat from trays on our laps on the sofa, where our knees will practically be touching.

"Fuck me," I mumble under my breath as I walk back

home. I could at least wait until the fire breaks out before I start running for the hydrant.

The first thing I notice as I make my way up the back stairs to my place is that the music appears to have stopped. The next is an incredible smell.

Confused, I hurry up the last few steps and jam my key into the door. Upon entering, however, I immediately stop, bowled over by the adorable sight that greets me.

Jessie is sound asleep on the sofa, wrapped up in my favorite blue blanket, with half of my cats curled up around him. He's clearly vacuumed and tidied, but that's not what's threatening to make my heart stop.

He's wearing sparkly cat ears. I guess they're on some kind of headband as they're poking out from his dark curls. Whatever the case, it's stirring something within me that I haven't felt in a long time.

Closing the door, I realize that I can definitely smell something absolutely delicious. I rush into the kitchen, and sure enough, there's a lasagna bubbling away in the oven. I hastily pull it out, seeing that it's a little crispy around the edges, but otherwise, it looks heavenly.

No offense to my veggie stir fry, but that pales in comparison to a vat of pasta, meat, and cheese. I inhale the scent deeply, then place the dish down on a heatproof mat for it to cool. My heart feels like it's going to burst out of my chest. Jessie did this for us?

For me?

I'm supposed to be the one taking care of him, but I can't remember the last time someone cooked me a meal. There's an odd lump in my throat that I struggle to swallow down.

What an absolute sweetheart.

And now he's sound asleep on my sofa. He's probably more than exhausted after everything he's been through. Knowing I can reheat the lasagna at any time, I decide that he needs rest more than anything. So I head back into the living room and gently start shooing cats away from him so I can take him upstairs.

"Come on, Saggie," I grumble, picking up a particularly stubborn little guy who refuses to move. "I know he's your new best friend, but he has to move now."

Sagittarius glowers at me and flicks his tail, but he waits by my feet, probably working out that he can follow me in a second. Some of these cats are just too smart for their own good.

Before tending to my new house guest, I pick his phone off the floor and pocket it before leaning down to reach for my sleepy kitty. I try and keep the blanket wrapped around him as I pick him up in a bridal carry. But it slips as I lift him and…oh…dear…*god*. He's only got tiny shorts on and half a T-shirt. Well, he's also got socks and paw slippers on his feet, but that's not really the issue here.

He's so adorable and half-naked and *gah!*

Okay, the only solution is to put him back down again as quickly as possible. He's pretty heavy despite being so small. I can feel how muscular he is. But I manage to get him up the stairs without rousing him. A parade of kitties follows us into his bedroom, but that's no surprise to me. They already love the hell out of him.

He's unpacked in here, and seeing his teddies and other knick-knacks in my space makes my heart flip in my chest. I hate how much I love it. But I can't get used to it. That way leads to danger.

As I go to place him on the bed so I can let him go, he rolls in closer to me, nuzzling his face against my chest and clinging to my arms with a moan.

I freeze.

"Jessie?" I say softly. "It's bedtime now."

He sighs with a little puff of air. "Okay, Nim," he mumbles

sleepily, allowing me to ease him from my grip and onto the mattress. Somehow I yank the duvet back, but before he can burrow under the covers completely, I pull off his slippers.

Tucking him in, I can't seem to stop myself from reaching out and brushing a wayward curl from his forehead. Then I snatch my hand back, knowing I've crossed a line. Stepping back, I watch as several kitties jump up to join him. Usually, they fight for a spot on my bed or occupy the tree perches in my room. I have a suspicion that tonight I'm going to feel a little lonely.

But that's okay. Jessie is all that matters.

I creep back downstairs, then take a second to rest against the wall and massage the ache in my chest.

He's perfect. He's beautiful. He's kind and hardworking, and he's a *god damned kitten.*

"Really, universe?" I say, looking toward the heavens. "What have I done to deserve this torment?"

CHAPTER 9

Jessie

It takes about three seconds after I wake up before panic explodes in my chest.

Where the fuck am I?

I gasp and flail. It's only when I send several cats scattering across the dark room do I start to remember what's going on.

Nim.

I'm at his place. This is my new room, and these are some of his cats that were keeping me company. But…hang on. This isn't right. I didn't fall asleep here, did I? And why am I half naked? A loud rumble from my stomach also reminds me that I'm starving. My phone is on the nightstand, so I check the time and see it's just before eight at night. Wait… wasn't I…?

"The lasagna!" I shriek. Tumbling from the bed, I go to run out of the room. But at the last second, I spin around and grab a hoodie so I don't feel quite as exposed. If the house is on fire, then I'll have a lot of cats to save, and I'd rather not face the firefighters in little more than a bra and panties.

But as I run down the stairs I don't see or smell any

smoke. My heart is still racing as I skid into the kitchen, looking frantically around. The oven is off. Did I dream making dinner in the first place?

"Thank you," a low voice rumbles behind me. I shriek again and spin around, clutching my chest.

Nim is standing in the doorway, looking sheepish with his hands in his pockets.

"Oh, fuck," I splutter. "Sorry, I'm still half-asleep. Um, thank you for what?"

He juts his chin toward the fridge. "Lasagna. And cleaning up."

I blink at him before stepping over and opening the fridge door to peek inside. Sure enough, there's the dish I made minus a square. I bite my lip, trying to piece my memories together.

"Oh…no," I say, feeling the blush creep onto my face as embarrassment sweeps through me. "I fell asleep on the sofa, didn't I? Why didn't my alarm wake me up?" I snatch my phone out of my pocket and open my clock app. Sure enough, I set the time.

I just never pressed start, apparently.

I look up at Nim in horror. "I could have burned your apartment down," I utter. "And the café. Holy fuck, I put *all the cats in danger—*"

"Hey, hey," Nim says quickly, closing the distance as I start to spiral. Before I know it, his arms are wrapped around me, hugging me tightly. I cling to him, trying to breathe properly. But tears are spilling from my eyes as I imagine how much of a disaster I could have caused.

How many lives I could have destroyed.

"I'll leave," I choke out. "I'll pack my stuff right now and—"

"Jessie, *stop*," Nim barks. He moves to hold my shoulders and looks into my eyes. I hiccup, but miraculously, I do stop crying like he said. "It was an accident. Nothing bad happened."

"It could have," I insisted.

He shrugs and steps back. I miss his touch immediately. "But it didn't."

I swallow and rub the back of my neck. "Right," I say slowly. Gradually, my heartbeat starts to slow down. However, now I'm feeling completely awkward as we just stand there and look at each other, various cats twining around our legs. "Um, so, you liked the lasagna?"

He grunts, that ghost of a smile twitching at the corner of his mouth again. "Yeah. Thanks. It was…yeah. Thanks."

I know words are not his forte, so I take what he says at face value that he really did enjoy it. "You're welcome. Do you think…do you mind if I have some? I haven't eaten today, and I didn't want to just steal your food for myself, but I thought it might be nice to make dinner for the both of us, but then I fell asleep and…"

"Course," he says with a frown, stepping over to the fridge and removing the dish so he can cut another square out and put it in a glass bowl with a lid. "You want it hot?"

I move across the kitchen and lean against a counter. "Yes, please. Thank you."

He shoves it into the microwave and jabs at the buttons, leaving us with a background hum as it starts to cook.

"Uhh…" I say, anxious to break the tension between us. "I'm sorry I fell asleep and almost burned your home down. I know you told me to stop apologizing, but I feel like this is a pretty good exception. Also, I could have sworn I passed out on the couch, so, um…do you know anything about that?"

He shrugs and looks at the microwave for a few moments, making me think he's going to tell me I sleep-walked up the stairs, or not even answer at all.

"You needed proper sleep," he mumbles.

I continue to frown. "But how did I—"

"Carried you," he cuts me off.

For a second, I just stare. It's his turn for his face to turn pink. "You…carried me up the stairs without waking me up?" I ask.

"You were really tired," he says without meeting my eyes, like that explains everything.

I'm so stunned I don't know what to say. This man, who I met literally hours ago, was so worried about me that he carried me like some sort of superhero upstairs and tucked me into bed?

A lump rises in my throat, and my eyes sting. I blink furiously, refusing to cry. It's difficult because I'm feeling so many emotions all at once. Mostly, I just feel so *treasured.* Like I matter. Don't get me wrong. My mom loves me to the moon and back. I've never doubted that. But she's been through so much over the past five years it didn't leave her which much energy to give me a whole lot of attention. And anyway, the kind of affection I've been craving really wasn't the maternal kind.

I've been dreaming of a man who thinks the world of me. Who will anticipate my needs and—just every once in a while—do something sweet.

I've known Nim for half a day and he's made me feel like some sort of Disney princess.

Mercifully, the timer beeps on the microwave, pulling us from the pregnant pause that had fallen over the room. I shake myself and smile, catching Nim's eye again. "Wow, that does smell good, if I do say so myself."

He grunts with that little smile again. "Tastes even better," he says, making me glow with pride.

He scoops the generous, steaming portion onto a plate, and sets it on a tray. But then he gets a bowl and tips some salad into it from a bag. He fetches some ranch dressing from the fridge, and holds it up, raising his eyebrows at me.

"Oh, yes, please," I say, watching as he pours some over the green leaves. Then he butters a roll. "Is all that for me?" I ask hesitantly.

"You said you haven't eaten all day," he answers with a scowl.

I bite my lip. "Yes, but it's your food. I don't want to be greedy."

He looks up at me, and I swear his grumpy demeanor softens ever so slightly. "You can have whatever," he grunts firmly. "Don't be shy."

Before I can really process his words, he takes the tray and marches into the living room. Looking around at the various cats still with me, I grimace at them. "I suppose I should follow, huh?" I whisper.

When they start walking toward the living room, I take that as my cue to do the same.

Nim is waiting for me, standing by the sofa. When I enter, I'm rewarded with a fractionally bigger smile. "Sit," he says, almost proudly. It's like...he's enjoying fussing over me. Perhaps I don't have to feel like such a terrible burden after all?

Making sure I don't disturb any kitties, I make my way over and sink down onto the couch. He places the tray on the coffee table, picks up the nice blue blanket, and drapes over my bare legs.

My heart flips in my chest. Whoa. That's...intimate.

But he plods on like it's nothing unusual, turning to fetch the tray again and settling it on my lap. He walks around the back of the sofa so he can go sit on the other end. It's not huge, and I feel like we're suddenly quite close. But he doesn't seem to notice, so I try my best to ignore it.

He picks up the TV remote and unfreezes the screen. He

must have paused it when I shrieked myself awake earlier. An image of some kind of bird flying through the sky comes back to life, and I assume it must be a nature documentary.

"This okay?" Nim asks me.

"Uh, sure," I reply without even really thinking. It's his home, after all. I'll watch whatever he likes. Apart from scary horror movies. I hate those. Typically, I like trashy reality TV shows and competitions, but I imagine he's more interested in animals than people.

Unable to fight my growling stomach any longer, I pick up my fork and attack the lasagna I poured my heart into earlier that day. Even reheated in the microwave, it's still damned good, and I can't help but moan as I drag the cutlery from my lips.

My eyes snap to him, though. He's staring, but he looks away quickly. Great, I'm making us both embarrassed. *Just shut up and eat, Jessie.*

It's not so hard to do. With all the drama yesterday, I didn't have much of a dinner then either, and once I start eating, I can't stop. The pasta soon vanishes, and I don't pause before tackling the side salad or the bread roll. I feel much better after that.

Without saying anything (naturally), Nim takes the tray from me and heads back out to the kitchen, leaving me with a pack of hyenas on the screen that has some of the cats very interested indeed with all the strange noises they're making. I'm so busy watching the various different kitties that I'm taken by surprise as Nim plops back onto the sofa. He's still got the tray I was using, but this time he puts it between us.

Now it's holding a tub of ice cream with two spoons sticking out.

He juts his chin and grunts, and I'm confident he's telling me to help myself. Looking down, I see that the flavor is butter pecan, one of my favorites. "Thank you!" I squeak earnestly, grabbing one of the spoons.

I'm trying not to get carried away, but this is so cute and cozy. Yeah, I know my new friend is a slightly terrifying-looking tattooed biker. But my mom taught me to judge actions, not appearances, and he has been so insanely kind to me today I can't stop my heart from melting like the ice cream.

If I'm being honest, this dinner has felt more like a date than anything Parker and I ever did together. I'm starting to appreciate that I just liked the idea of him more than who he actually was. I was blinded by sex, but I have to wonder now if that was any good either or if it was just good because it was better than my right hand.

I'm soon yanked from my thoughts as I scratch my head and realize with absolute horror that I've had the cat-ear headband on this whole time.

"Oh, shit," I yelp before I can stop myself. I drag the thing off my head and shove it into the front pouch pocket of my hoodie. "That's embarrassing."

Nim frowns and shrugs, not meeting my eye. "You should feel at home here," he says simply.

"Yeah, but that's kind of a private thing," I start babbling, knowing I'm blushing yet again. "I don't want you to think I'm weird. It's just like, uh, a comfort thing, I guess. Like a blankie. I know I'm too old for shit like that, but after the past few years and my mom's illness, I don't really care about what other people think of that kind of stuff anymore, you know? Like, if it's not hurting anyone else, why does it matter? But I didn't mean to make you feel awkward or anything."

He licks his lips and glances quickly over at me. "You didn't. I'm sorry about your mom."

"Oh, she's fine now," I say. "I mean, the cancer's gone.

Something like that takes a bit of time to get over psychologically, though. For both of us. But health-wise, she's in remission. We'll have to wait a few years to really be sure, but there's every hope it's all gone. Thank you all the same!" God, I'm so ungrateful. And awkward. Did I mention awkward?

He nods. "Good." Then he chews on his lip and appears to steel himself before speaking again. "Don't hide the ears on my account. They suit you."

Whoa.

Blood rushes to my face, but it's an entirely different feeling than before. His words are warmer to me than the blanket wrapped around my legs. For a moment, I'm too stunned to reply. Eventually, though, I remember my manners and do my best to stop the awkwardness from growing.

"Thank you," I say softly.

Does he really mean it? The idea of being myself around him is so liberating and…well, after today, is it crazy that I trust him? Like, for real trust that I can be vulnerable around him? He's already saved me twice in a matter of hours. First from sleeping in my car and then when he came back in time to rescue the lasagna.

Maybe I'm totally naïve, and this is going to come back and bite me in the ass. But for now, I slip the headband out of my hoodie pouch and place it back on my head before reaching for my ice cream spoon again. As I go to scoop a little from the carton, I catch Nim's gaze, and his smile might still be small, but it's definitely fond.

Yes. I think I've made a real friend.

And I'm so, so happy about it.

CHAPTER 10

Jessie

AT SOME POINT, I JUST STOP QUESTIONING EVERYTHING ALL the time. Yes, this whole situation is slightly bizarre and happened super fast. I'm still avoiding telling my mom all the details. It's almost like if I confess to her, the bubble will burst, and it won't be real anymore. Or maybe by telling someone else, I'll realize how insane it all is.

The bottom line is that I'm safe, and actually, I'm already thriving.

For the first several days, I get into a pretty nice routine just looking after the cats both in Nim's apartment and in the café. I'm fully aware that scooping out oopsies from litter boxes and washing food bowls aren't the most glamorous jobs, but I love knowing that the kitties are clean and cared for. They rely on us humans for everything, after all.

I'm getting to know their personalities better, especially all the black ones in the apartment. I like how Virgo is such a scaredy cat, but if you sit still and let him come to you, he'll actually let me stroke him and he'll purr in his little heart out in my lap. Aries, on the other hand, is an absolute bruiser who isn't afraid of anything, but when she rolls onto her back, she genuinely wants tummy pets, and that's sweet in a different way.

I love them all. Nim is lucky to have them. A little voice in the back of my head tells me not to get too attached as I'll only have to leave them all one day. But I just can't bring myself to listen.

When my classes start, I suddenly have a lot less free time, which is probably a good thing. There's a strange sort of tension when both Nim and I are around. Obviously, he's at work a lot of the time, and when he's not I'm fully aware that this is his home and I want to respect that. I try to make myself scarce in my room, but he's got this thing about making sure I eat enough, so we often share meals. It's incredibly sweet, but at the same time a little intimidating.

I'm torn between wanting to be around him and not. Because I *love* spending as much time with him as possible. I don't think either of us is sure when this arrangement of ours is going to come to an end, and I want to make the most out of it that I can.

On the other hand, I'm not really certain *what* is going on. He seems to really enjoy fussing over me, and I'm becoming addicted to that, too. But then it's like he realizes what he's doing and suddenly pulls back, like I might change my mind without warning and start hating him for it or something. I just don't know.

That's why going to class helps considerably. Suddenly, my head is full of a million new things, and I have very little time left to fret over the relationship dynamic between my new friend and me. Between philosophy, English lit, and art history, I barely have time to catch my breath. It's been a long while since I applied my brain to a classroom, and by the time I fall into bed each night, I'm exhausted.

All things considered, maybe adding a serious extracurricular activity on top of that might not be the smartest move. But cheerleading is in my blood. Mom was a cheerleader back at her school and college, and she made me promise that I wouldn't give up on my dreams just because the big C came along and messed with both our plans. Besides, Paddle Creek's squad is called the Kittens. That feels like far too big of a sign from the universe to ignore.

Still, when Saturday rolls around for tryouts, I find myself standing outside the gymnasium, rooted to the spot in fear.

What if this isn't who I am anymore? What if I'm no good? I've spent five years trying to find my way back to this point, but what if it's all a big mistake? What if—?

"Hi!"

I jerk from my reverie and find a beaming girl next to me in a purple hoodie as well as a purple-and-teal skirt sticking out the bottom. With a rush I realize she must be an existing Kitten, and I feel like I'm standing in front of royalty or something ridiculous. It's not like this squad is renowned for winning championships or anything. I just…oh, gosh. I just want so badly to *belong* to something again. To have a purpose bigger than myself.

"Hi!" I squeak. "I, um…" I point toward the building. "Tryouts?"

She laughs, but it's kind. "Absolutely, baby! You cheered before?"

To my surprise, she loops her arm through mine and begins marching us toward the gym. It makes me feel claimed, and a warm sensation unfurls inside me. "Oh, yeah," I manage to say. "In high school, but I took some time off."

"I'm sure you'll do great," she says fondly as we go inside. "I'm Zazzle, by the way."

"Jessie," I say with a shy smile.

Zazzle's long dark braids have purple woven into them. She's also got a couple of tattoos I can see on her bare legs, as well as several empty piercing holes in her ears. A small

Band-Aid covers one on her tragus that I assume she can't or doesn't want to take out, and the stud in her nose is very small, but I can see it up close like this.

"We don't have a lot of boy Kittens," she says jovially as we walk through the slightly dingy hallway.

I hesitate for a second. But for some reason, being in a new place with new people gives me courage. "Actually, I'm a demiboy," I say.

"Oh, interesting," she says earnestly. "What does that mean? What pronouns do you use?"

"He, him, his," I tell her with a smile. "It just means that for me, being a boy includes a lot of femininity. It's different for everyone, I guess, but that's the label that feels best for me."

"Hey, you don't have to justify anything to me," she says as she holds up her hands. "It's all good, cutie. We might be a small squad with just one team, but you'll find quite a lot of diversity here in Paddle Creek."

"Yeah?" I ask. Some of my nerves are being replaced with curiosity. I'm grateful to this girl I just met.

She nods with a grin. "The Kittens might be a little… uh…well, we're enthusiastic, but we don't exactly have a lot of trophies," she says with a chuckle. "The Panthers, though? Our football team. They're pretty damn great. Won state a few times. And their coach is openly gay. It attracts a lot of queer players to the team and therefore the college in general. And the town. Have you been to Creams yet?"

I arch an eyebrow at her. "Creams?"

"The Ice Cream Parlor," she explains as we approach a double door. "The best gay bar in a fifty-mile radius."

Something shivers within me. I might be twenty-three and done my fair share of drinking, but I've never actually been to a bar or a club, let alone a queer one. Of course

Parker never mentioned it, probably because he didn't want to have to make up excuses as to why we couldn't go there.

The usual flash of rejection cuts through me, but I'm surprised at how it's already duller compared to the previous week. Instead, I wonder if Nim knows about this place. I can't exactly see him hanging out somewhere like that, but he might have some local knowledge he could pass on to me. Thinking about him makes me feel warm, too. But it's also complicated, so I try and forget about it for now.

As soon as we walk through the doors into the gym, the nerves come back with a vengeance. My hand immediately flies to my mouth, and I start nibbling on my thumbnail.

The room is split into two different groups. Those wearing a mixture of purple-and-teal hoodies, T-shirts, shorts, and bows, and those in regular clothes. It's almost half and half. My stomach drops, and I turn to Zazzle.

"How many spaces do you have to fill?" I ask.

"Oh, everyone gets on the game-day squad," she says breezily. "Cheering for the Panthers is super fun. But, um, there are only three openings on the competition squad." She briefly looks apologetic, but then she squeezes my arm with a little squeal. "Honestly, a lot of people start on game day before making it to comp. We train together and have a lot of socials, so everyone feels included. I'm sure you'll do great!"

I bite my lip and look around again. She's right. I'm the only guy trying out, and there are just four in uniform compared to around twenty girls. That makes a difference if I want to fly again. But I'm getting ahead of myself. I haven't even set foot on the mat yet.

"How many competitions do you do a year?" I ask.

"In theory…three regionals and then grand nationals in Nashville in spring," Zazzle says brightly. However, I hear the 'but' before it even reaches her mouth. "But we rarely raise enough money to actually *get* to nationals. We do the Cheer

First program, so we don't have to qualify at regionals to go further. But winning a smaller comp or even coming in the top three would probably go a long way to getting sponsorship. I haven't made it there yet."

She shakes herself and laughs.

"Wow, sorry. You don't need to know all that. Honestly, what matters is being a Kitten. It's a family. We don't need trophies and medals and stuff."

I see the wistful look in her eyes. "Although…they might be nice every once in a while?" I suggest.

She laughs again and pats my back. "Maybe. Why don't I let you warm up? Good luck out there!"

I give the air a soft punch. "Go Kittens," I say weakly.

"That's it!"

She runs off, waving to a bunch of her teammates who are sitting on the bleachers. I inhale slowly, then let it out. "Okay," I whisper to myself. "You can do this."

I went for a run before I arrived here to warm up my muscles, so I drop my bag and get right to stretching, drinking half my bottle of water in an attempt to keep my mouth from drying out. Some of the girls seem to know each other and are chatting happily. A lot of them have the same high ponytail and sparkly bow, wearing little more than a crop top and shorts vibe, which I'm used to. And obviously, if that's how they feel comfortable, that's great. It's what works for me, after all.

But then there's a pale redheaded girl with a pixie cut, wearing a faded My Chemical Romance tee and knee-length shorts who catches my eye. The others seem to be giving her a wide birth. That's all the invitation I need to wander closer as I circle my shoulders and rock my head back and forth.

"Hey," I say with a dorky wave, immediately followed by an internal eye roll. Yeah, I wouldn't want to be friends with me, either.

To my surprise, pixie girl's face lights up with a smile. "Hey! Are you trying out?" She then does her eye roll out loud. "Of course you are. Why else would you be standing in front of me stretching? I'm Alannah."

She sticks out her hand and I gladly take it. "Jessie," I reply.

"Nice to meet you," she says with a cheeky wink. "Hey, did you see that the hoodies have ears on the top? How cool is that? I heard that one of the girl's moms hand sews them on. I think that's adorable."

"Or tacky, depending on your taste levels," someone says from behind us. We both turn to see a stunningly pretty tall girl with impressive blonde curls giving us a tight smile that doesn't reach her eyes. She's holding a clipboard and pen. "But apparently, we all have to look the same for 'team spirit' or something. Names?"

I blink for a second, composing myself. Yikes. Is this the captain? "Uh, Jessie Garras," I say before remembering to smile.

"Alannah Connick. That's Alannah with the 'h,' in case you were wondering."

"Tara," the girl replies. "Without the 'h,' in case you were wondering."

She might still be smiling, but I catch the slight hint of mockery as she parrots back Alannah's words to her. Before either of us can react, she ticks twice on the clipboard list, then moves on with much higher enthusiasm to some of the other more traditional-looking cheerleaders.

"Huh," I say.

"That doesn't feel like a good sign," Alannah says.

"No, it does not," I agree.

Before we can fret too much, a whistle is blown from in front of the bleachers. I turn to see a middle-aged woman in a white polo shirt and black slacks waving everyone over to her. She's wearing thick black glasses and has an unruly bob of brown hair down to her shoulders. The way she places her hands on her hips and sighs as we crowd around her makes me think that this woman is very tired indeed.

In contrast, a tiny Asian girl with glittery teal eye shadow stands beside her, rocking on the balls of her feet, apparently barely able to contain her excitement.

"She's the captain," Alannah whispers to me. That's a relief. But I'm still wary as I watch Tara swan over and stand beside them.

"Okay! All right," says the woman in a loud voice that has us all paying attention. "Welcome to cheerleader tryouts. If you're here for baseball, you're in the wrong room."

Her joke gets a weak ripple of laughter. She sighs and shakes her head.

"Right. I am Professor Ulman. I am here to make sure that nobody breaks anything, and if you *do* break something that happens to be on a human being, I'm here to call 911. Thank you all for filling out your details in advance for insurance purposes. Now, while I go grade papers, I shall leave you in the capable hands of your brand-new captain..." Her face goes blank, and she glances at the tiny girl beside her.

"Lakelyn Jones," she whispers.

"Lakelyn Jones!" cries Professor Ulman. "So good luck and uh...try really hard *not* to break anything, 'kay?" She gives us two thumbs up and a hopeful look before spinning around and trudging back toward the back of the bleachers.

Lakelyn, on the other hand, skips up to Tara and happily takes the clipboard, then skips back to center stage, beaming at all us newbies. The current members of the squad are all sitting behind her on the bleachers, but I can see that there are a guy and a girl on the front row also with clipboards. Zazzle joins them, as does Tara. I get the feeling they must be the committee.

Okay, so if it's them and the captain I need to impress, at least one of them already knows my name and smiled at me. That might not mean anything in the long run, but at least it gives me a little extra confidence when one of them also seemed less than friendly.

"Hey, y'all," the tiny captain says with a strong Southern accent. "I'm Coach El, and I'll be running your tryouts today. So the important thing to know is that there's room for everyone to be a game-day Kitten. Goooo Panthers!"

A few of the new girls scream and clap, making me wonder if their boyfriends are on the team. Maybe that's unfair, but in my experience, there are often a couple of girls who still only want to be a cheerleader to either get a new boyfriend or hang out with their current one.

If that's what makes them happy, good for them. I only like going to games if the players aren't douchebags. What I'm here for is to compete.

Lakelyn claps and jumps until the newbies calm down, then continues with her welcome speech. "Some of you have indicated that you're interested in the competition squad, and that's great! We only have a few spots available right now, but we always need reserves, and trust me, we'll still be stunting at the games."

Beside me, Alannah cracks her knuckles. I'm guessing she's interested in competing as well. "You a base?" I lean over and ask quietly. She nods, and I look her up and down. "I reckon we're the same height. You want to pair up for group stunt?"

Her eyes go wide. "Hell yeah," she whispers back, and we share a quiet high five.

Lakelyn is still talking. "So first off, we'll learn a little choreo, including a jump sequence that we'll perform in groups. After that, we'll spend some time stunting with the current Kittens. I'll rotate people in and out so we can get a good sense of what you're capable of. Finally, when we're nice and tired, you can show me who can tumble. In fact—who's got a front or back handspring?"

Several of the girls raise their hand, as do I. Alannah stiffens beside me. "Uh, I can cartwheel," she murmurs, but I don't think anyone else hears. My heart sinks for her. Different levels require different gymnastics, I know. But for the teams I grew up on, cheer and gymnastics were always intertwined.

"Great," Lakelyn says genuinely. "And any tucks?"

Most of the others put their hands down. In fact, it's only me and one other girl who don't. Rather than feel good about this, I sense several eyes narrowing on me, including Tara's. Not Lakelyn, though.

"Oh, wow. Nice! Okay, we'll look forward to seeing those later. Right now, let's dance!"

I finally lower my hand and reach over to squeeze Alannah's shoulder. "Hey, don't sweat it," I tell her. "Not everyone needs to be a tumbler."

She sighs. "Yeah, but it helps on the competition floor, doesn't it?"

Soon, though, we're in the thick of learning the short bit of choreography. It's only eight counts of eight, but I'm surprised how fast Alannah picks it up. She's a fantastic dancer, moving with real confidence and sass that makes me grin. However, her jumps aren't all that great, and my heart pangs for her chances.

Zazzle and the other two Kittens are whooping and clapping for everyone. But Tara seems to have her own little clique sitting behind her that doesn't look impressed by anyone other than the pretty, long-haired tumbler who had her hand up with me. She looks like she'd match their aesthetic nicely.

Alannah and me—not so much.

Still, when we get to stunting, I manage to stick with my new redheaded friend like I promised, and we get an experienced flyer to work with, easily throwing up extended one- and two-foot shapes.

As our flyer is about to load for a basket toss, someone snaps, "Move!" It's Tara. She gives us that same tight smile as she switches places with our back, wrapping her hands around the flyer's waist. "Let's see what you've got, then."

"Uh, sure," I say, giving Alannah a confident nod before looking back at the flyer. "We still good to do an X out with a double twist down?"

"No problem," says our flyer as she grips tightly onto our shoulders.

I glance at Tara. "Do you want to call it or should I—?"

"One, two, down, up!" Tara calls without warning. The flyer jumps, still holding our shoulders, and it's a testament to Alannah and me that we grab onto each other's wrists quickly enough so they're interlocked underneath the flyer's feet.

Damn. I try not to get rattled, but Lakelyn is watching, and Tara obviously isn't going to make this easy for us.

"Ready?" Lakelyn asks, her clipboard up and her pen poised and ready.

"Ready!" we cry together.

This time, I'm ready for Tara's "One, two, down, up!" and we fling the flyer upward.

I watch her like a hawk as she executes a beautiful X-shape with her body before twisting in the air. In theory, she'll rotate twice before landing in a cradle position in my and Alannah's outstretched arms with Tara bracing the backs of her shoulders.

But that doesn't happen.

"Careful!" Tara yells, spooking the girl in the air. She jerks and Alannah and I end up catching her on her side in a tangle of limbs. Tara hasn't got her back at all. In fact, she's stepped away from the stunt entirely.

For some reason, she rounds on Alannah. "What were you thinking?" she snaps.

We let the poor flyer down gently before addressing Tara. "What?" Alannah says back in confusion.

"You're the one who shouted," I insist.

Tara turns her icy blue eyes on me. "Because you weren't in the right position."

"We were fine until you yelled at us," I contend hotly. "And you moved back and didn't catch her."

"Okay, okay," Lakelyn says, waving her hands. "Is everyone all right?"

We nod. I notice Professor Ulman has stood up with her hand on her chest, grimacing as she looks at us.

Great. Now she thinks we're a liability.

Lakelyn says it's all fine and she's seen enough anyway, but I'm fuming. Tara has already slunk off, but it's clear she's got it in for my new friend.

"Fuck her," I mumble into Alannah's ear.

"No, thank you," she mumbles back. "I have standards."

Despite everything else going on, that warms my heart. After what Zazzle said, I was sure I wasn't going to feel alone on the squad, but I'm even happier if Alannah is queer.

"We haven't got long left," Lakelyn is telling the wannabe Kittens. "So let's tumble. Show us what you've got, even if it's something simple. Do a cartwheel with style. We can still use that."

I noticed earlier we've only got gym mats under our feet, no sprung floor. God, it's been so long since I trained properly. I managed to get down the rec center back home this summer to brush off some skills, but right now, I'm still nervous.

Alannah, though, has fight in her eyes. We're allowed to

organize ourselves in a line, and she chooses to go near the front. When it's her turn, she manages a half decent cartwheel but finishes it off with some feisty spirit moves and the biggest grin like she just won the Olympics.

"Yeah! You go, baby!" I bellow as most other people clap enthusiastically for her effort.

But then I find myself dropping back and letting everyone else go before me as I chew on my thumbnail and fret.

What do I do? Something basic that I know I can land? Or something hardcore to wipe the smirk off Tara's face? No, I want to get on the competition squad. It's better to rein it in and not be so flashy. After almost two hours with this team, I can tell that they have a lot of heart but they're not very advanced. We'll be competing in a lower division, so my more advanced running tumbles won't be legal anyway. Best not to be the new guy who shows off.

Expect when there's no one else left to go and I step up, I see Tara out of the corner of my eye whispering to her cohorts. They all look me up and down and sneer like I'm little more than dirt on their shoes.

O,h *hell* no.

Spite and fury rush through me, and before I know what I'm doing, my feet are sprinting across the floor.

I launch myself into the air with a round-off into a bank handspring. And another. And another. Followed by a full twisting layout, ending by coming back the way I came with a cheeky front tuck. I stamp my feet onto the mat, sticking the landing right in the middle in front of the committee, my fists clenched so tightly that my fingernails are biting into my palms. I grit my teeth and glare directly at Tara.

There's a moment where nobody moves a muscle. It's Alannah who suddenly roars and claps with Zazzle a split second behind her. The rest of the room explodes, and several people run over to me, including Lakelyn, whose eyes are shining. "Jessie, that was incredible," she says breathlessly.

I notice Tara and her cronies are clapping politely, but her expression is dangerous.

Chances are high that I'm going to pay for that sooner rather than later. I don't know how, but in that moment, with the adrenaline pumping through me, I'm arrogant enough not to care.

Right now, I just want to get home and tell Nim all about it. That's a dangerous rush all by itself. But much like the tumble pass I just pulled, I can't bring myself to regret it.

CHAPTER 11

Nim

I'm going out of my mind.

I meant what I said about Jessie being comfortable here and wearing what he wants. This is his home, at least for the time being. He needs space to be authentic, especially while he's adjusting to his new class schedule and waiting to hear back from the cheerleading squad. His energy is all very fractious.

However, I'm becoming more and more convinced that he doesn't even really know that he's a kitten in the kinky sense or what that really means for him on several levels. He certainly has *no fucking clue* what he's doing to me.

Every day it's the kitten ears, tiny shorts, and half a T-shirt. All I can see is long, creamy limbs and the way his muscles flex and stretch when he moves. There's a happy trail on his defined stomach that draws my gaze down to forbidden territory. When he puts his headphones on so as not to disturb me with his music, those have kitten ears on as well, for heaven's sake. He twirls and sings under his breath and generally brings sunshine into my world.

How did I live before him? How will I manage when he's gone? I'm not just talking about how he does more than his fair share of chores around the apartment. I'm talking about me. He's the first thing I think of when I wake up and the last thing I check on before I go to sleep. The cats split themselves between us at night. How sad are they going to be when their uncle Jessie moves on?

Of course I'm coping with this influx of complicated feelings by hiding from him as much as possible. Because I know a big part of what I'm experiencing is just good old-fashioned lust. It's been forever since Brent, and hook-ups don't really do it for me. I like to feel a connection to the person I'm intimate with. Besides, Paddle Creek was the last place I expected to find a kitten falling into my lap.

I came here because it was where a lot of my chapter had settled down. I didn't really put two and two together that queer bikers might make a town queer. Or that they might have chosen the place because it was already open and accepting. The football coach being out and proud really has been a big influence around these parts.

Whatever the case, the result is the same. I actually *did* have the prettiest kitty boy fall into my lap, and now with very little effort, he's falling into my heart. All I want is for him to be happy and healthy. It's my all-consuming mission. And the way his face lights up when I surprise him with food or appear with a blanket for him?

Priceless.

Right now, though. I'm in danger of wrestling him to the floor and pinning him there so he'll *stop* pacing the living room.

Admittedly, he's behind me as I sit on the sofa, trying to watch TV. But I can feel him moving and hear him whispering along to whatever obnoxiously cheerful pop song he's got blasting into his ears. His cat paw slippers are scuffing on the floor, and occasionally, he snaps his fingers in time to the beat only he can hear.

He's just so...*present*. He's everywhere. My cats' eyes follow him as he walks up and down, their heads bobbing and their tails swishing. I can't forget about him, even if I try.

Today is a Monday—my Saturday, essentially, as I have both Mondays and Tuesdays off. Usually, I'd wander down to the café anyway or volunteer at the rescue shelter where the café fosters its cats from. However, both this week and last week, I've found myself unable to leave the apartment. It seems such a terrible waste of my time with Jessie. But beyond cooking for him I'm not really sure how best to spend time with him. He's so...sparkly and sweet. I doubt he'd want to hang out with me.

And yet he's still here. I know he doesn't have any classes for the rest of the day, as he told me so. I'm positive he's made new friends already. In fact, he told me he's become besties with a girl he met at the tryouts. They message all the time and have plans to go to that loud, shiny bar in town on Friday night.

But for now, he's still *here*.

With me.

Unable to stand it any longer, I turn on the couch and look at him. He stops in his tracks, looking chagrined as he yanks his headphones around his neck. Immediately, I can hear the tinny beat and voices that sound like chipmunks to me from over here.

"Oh, no," he says with a grimace. "I'm being annoying, aren't I?"

He's really not, so I shake my head. "Are you okay?" I ask pointedly.

Sighing, he pulls on his tail. Yes, *tail*. These small shorts have a glittery, fluffy, purply tail attached to his butt because apparently, he really does want to torture me to death.

"I'm just so worried about tryouts," he says glumly as he runs the soft material through his hands over and over. "I think it was bad I showed off."

I frown, genuinely confused. "Why wouldn't you show them your best?"

He shrugs and looks away. "One girl on the committee really didn't seem to like me. I don't know why."

I don't mean to be unkind, but I scoff and shake my head. "You're never gonna get everyone to like you. She sounds like a dick."

Thankfully, that gets a laugh from him, and some of the tension leaves his shoulders. "Yeah, she was a bit. Sorry. I know it's a stupid thing to obsess over. It's hardly life and death. I just miss competing and training and being a part of a team so much. Game day isn't the same. My whole life was cheerleading, and I just..."

"You want it back," I say, understanding. I felt so helpless when my family kicked me out. I was desperate to find something that was all mine so I could feel a sense of control again.

A thought crosses my mind.

It's a bad idea. I should be keeping my distance from Jessie, not encouraging anything further. Yet I can't seem to stop the words from tumbling from my mouth. Not a problem I usually have, I must admit.

"Come on," I grunt, getting to my feet and finding the remote so I can switch the TV off. "Get some clothes on. Uh...*more* clothes. Jeans."

He looks at me like I just started speaking in tongues, and I don't blame him. "Huh?"

I grab my keys from the bowl and my jacket off the peg on the wall. "We're going out."

"We are?" He shakes his head, then gives me a beautiful smile. "I mean, yeah! Sure! Okay! Let me just..." He looks down at himself. "Yeah...more clothes is probably a sensible idea. Give me a minute!"

He runs up the stairs with a couple of cats eagerly chasing after him. I deliberately try not to think about anything at all. Otherwise, I might change my mind and back out. Ultimately, what makes me stick with the plan is that I do believe that it's what's best for Jessie right now, and that's all that matters.

I might not be *his* Daddy, but I have committed to Daddying him. He needs this distraction.

There was a real risk he'd come back downstairs in a pair of heels and a fluffy crop top or something. But I'm pleased to see he's gone for jeans, sneakers, and a hoodie. Really, I should dress him head to toe in leathers, but I settle for giving him one of my jackets. It swamps him, but it's so adorable that I love it. So does he, apparently, from the way he grins at me after he shrugs it on.

"Does this mean what I think it means?" he asks.

I roll my eyes as I open the door, but I'm also smiling. "Come on, trouble," I grumble, ushering him outside.

He's practically dancing by the time we get down to the alley where my bike is parked. "Are we going for a ride?" he asks, skipping from one foot to the other.

My grin gets a little bigger. He seemed interested in the Harley-Davidson when I first showed it to him, but I was still a bit worried that he'd be afraid to actually try it out for himself. The open road is my passion. My escape when everything else in the world gets too much. To be able to share that with him?

Well, that feels really special right now.

"Just a short one," I warn him. "And not too fast. We're not wearing proper leathers. But I do have a helmet for you."

I keep the spare in my lockbox unless I know I'm going to need the space for luggage or anything. But it's ages since I took myself camping or anything like that. I haven't felt the inclination. It's funny how being with Jessie in this moment makes me feel like I might want to again sometime soon. But not today.

Today, we're going to introduce Jessie to what ninety-five horsepower and a hundred-and-twenty pound-feet of torque feels like between his thighs.

Part of my brain desperately wants to imagine what other kind of power might feel like between his thighs, but I shove those thoughts aside and throw my leg over the bike instead.

"Hop on," I tell him, flicking my eyes over my shoulder to indicate where I want him to sit. He eagerly jumps behind me and wraps his arms around my waist.

Dear lord, this might be a terrible idea. We haven't been this close since that first day when I couldn't stop myself from hugging him when he was becoming hysterical about the lasagna. But it's too late to back out now. He's so excited, and I'm not taking that away from him.

"Don't let go," I growl at him as I turn the ignition and kick the bike into life.

He meets my gaze with his ridiculously pretty brown eyes. "I won't," he says.

It sounds like a promise.

The traffic is reasonably light as we make our way out of the small town. This is a route I've taken many, many times. It's easy enough that I don't need any kind of map or GPS, not too far away so there's less time to get into any trouble, and usually the number of other cars is limited. It's just me and Jessie, taking on the trees and the sky.

"WOOHOO!" he yells at one point as we round a bend, climbing higher above the town. I'd never go so far as to call

this a mountain, but you could say it's a hill with big ambitions. It's not long before we come across the familiar rest-stop, so I pull the bike over and kill the engine. He's off the seat in a flash, pulling off his helmet and bopping around.

I pull my helmet off as well, and put them both in the lockbox. "You liked that, huh?" I say, unable to stop the smile that creeps onto my face.

"That was so, so cool! Thank you, Nim. This was so fun."

"Not there yet," I say smugly.

Trusting that he'll follow me, I turn and begin walking down a well-worn path that disappears into the foliage. There are aspens, elms, and oaks all around us, and their bark smells warm from the summer sunshine. A light breeze plays with the leaves, creating a rustling chorus. As soon as we step away from the road, it's so peaceful it feels like a little slice of heaven. I wonder if we'll see any cardinals.

"Where are we going?" Jessie asks cheekily as he walks beside me.

I raise an eyebrow and look down at him. "Wait and see," I grumble. Secretly, I love the way he's wriggling around with excitement. God, I want to do this all the time. I don't just want to prepare him meals and make sure he's clothed properly and sleeping comfortably.

I want to give him gifts and surprises and just generally see that look of wonder on his face that someone else has thought about him at all.

All I do is think about him.

Fuck, if he were mine and I could spoil him however I wanted, I'd buy him such nice tails and ears and toys and anything else his little kitten heart desired.

Maybe even a collar.

The thought brings me up short, although I barely falter in my step, and keep walking. I thought a lot about collaring

Brent, but it never felt like the right time. Thank goodness. That would have been a disaster. But with Jessie, the idea seems so natural. I bet he'd love it.

Only if it was what was right for him, though. With the right person. Honestly, that's probably not me, so I need to stop daydreaming about it right now.

My distraction comes quickly enough. The path we've been following has only one destination. All the paths around here do.

The Paddle Creek waterfall.

It's not very tall. In fact, if waterfalls are your thing, it's probably not that impressive at all. But the way Jessie gasps when he sees it tells me that he most likely feels the same way about it that I do.

"Oh my god," he whispers, covering his mouth with his hand as he takes in the sight. I'm so happy that, at least for now, we're all by ourselves and can enjoy the scene in private.

The creek flows down several shelves of purplish-gray slate rock into a large pool that eventually continues to travel downward toward the town. We're surrounded by trees, and bright August sunshine spills through the branches and dances on the rippling water. Unseen birds chirp and whistle, making the place feel truly alive.

Usually, I'm not so fussed to know what other people are thinking. That's their business. But right now, I'm dying to know what's going on in Jessie's head. "You like it?" I ask, folding my arms across my chest as if that might protect me from everything I'm feeling.

"Like it?" he splutters with a laugh. "I *love* it! It's so beautiful and alive and...and...it's like our own little kingdom we're surveying. Oh my god, can we get in the water?"

His question completely throws me. "Uh, people do, I guess. But it'll be cold—"

"That's the point," he cries, still laughing as he throws my jacket back to me and pulls his hoodie over his head.

He's not wearing anything underneath. Oh lord. I'd wondered many times before, but it turns out that his nipples are, in fact, pierced.

I'd worry that he hears my whimper, but he's too busy giggling to himself as he hops around removing his shoes and socks before shucking down his jeans.

For a heart-stopping moment I think he's going to go all the way and whip off his briefs as well. Mercifully, he stops there. But the bastard winks at me over his shoulder. "Are you coming?" he asks.

I'm too stunned to speak. Instead, I just watch on as he splashes into the water, shrieking and cackling at the cold.

But he does it, the crazy little minx. He takes a deep breath before falling over like a plank of wood, submerging under the water. My grip on the leather jacket in my hands tightens as I involuntarily take a step forward, my heart in my mouth. However, it's only a second before he emerges once more, flicking his hair and making a sparkling spray of water droplets that form a rainbow before my eyes.

There's a strong possibility that I might pass out.

"It's lovely!" he says through chattering teeth, waving me over. "Come on in!"

"No fucking chance," I grumble, but he can see that I'm smiling and shaking my head at his outrageousness. My heart is pounding, and I want to believe that it's just from the fear that his own heart might have stopped from the shock of that water. But my half-hard cock in my pants might indicate a different theory.

I'm saved from doing something really stupid by his phone pinging, suggesting he's received a message. His head immediately snaps to his jeans, where the device must be resting in his pocket.

"Fuck!" he yelps, already wading over. But I wave my hand and crouch down.

"Don't get out. You'll freeze."

"I have to get out at some point," he argues, but he does also stop where he is.

Good. I'm glad. He's having fun, and I don't want that to stop. Not yet, anyway.

"Let me get it for you," I insist.

He thinks about that for a second before nodding. I go over to his pile of clothes and fish inside his jeans pocket. "Who's it from?" he asks. "What does it say?"

"Unknown, and I can't tell beyond 'Dear Jessie, thank you so much for…'"

"FUCK!" he shrieks so loudly several birds take flight. "It's my tryout result! Hold the phone up so I can unlock it with my face."

For a second, I consider telling him to get out after all. I feel like this is his news, and if it's bad, he might want to react to it in private.

But then I decide to indulge him by coming closer to the pool. Selfishly, if it *is* bad news, then I want to comfort him. I don't want him to lock me out. I don't know if that's what his reaction would be, but I know that's what I'd do. So I take the easy way out and just do what he's told me to.

First, though, I place both our jackets down. Mine has my phone and keys in it, so if I slip, I won't fuck anything up in the water. Then I crouch down by the edge, and Jessie wades over so he's now exposed from the waist up. Water runs off his smooth, lithe body in rivets. I have to concentrate really hard to make sure I don't drop his phone.

The sensor obviously recognizes his face in a second, and then he's shaking his hand and blowing on his finger in what I assume is an effort to dry it. Because I'm an absolute sap, I offer the sleeve of my Henley.

"Use that," I tell him.

He does, holding my wrist with his other hand to steady himself. But then he keeps his grip on it as he starts tapping his phone, opening up the message, and reading it.

I don't have to wait long to find out the result.

"I'M IN!" he bellows to the high heavens, his eyes bugging out with shock and then tearing up with happiness. "I'm in! I made the competition squad! *ARGH!*"

"Well done, baby," I say with as much sincerity as I can muster in just three words. He gave up his dreams to take care of his mom, and I'm sure she's going to be just as proud as I am to hear that he's going to be competing again. He's a born cheerleader if I ever met one.

His hand is still wrapped around my wrist, and he's staring at me with his jaw hanging open. It's only then that my brain catches up to my tongue and I realize that I called him 'baby.'

Fuck.

I open my mouth to try and walk it back, but no words come. We're just staring intently at each other as he clings to me. His chest is rising and falling as his eyes search mine. I know I should regret it. This is exactly the kind of complication I've been trying to avoid.

But I can't run from the truth. Calling him 'baby' and 'kitten' and 'sweetheart' just feels so right. I want him to be all those things.

I want him to be mine.

Swallowing, I scramble for what to say. In that moment, it's as if we're locked together. There's something pulsing between us, heating up the air. My heart is racing, and try as I might, I can't tear my gaze away.

My head knows it's wrong. But my heart doesn't want to listen. He is my baby kitty. I'm his Daddy. In a way, we're already in too deep.

That's why when he suddenly yanks my wrist and his lips crash into mine, I stop fighting. I only just have the sense to toss the phone behind me before I'm falling into the water after him.

CHAPTER 12

Jessie

WE BOTH COME SPLUTTERING BACK UP TO THE SURFACE, AND Nim's looking at me in utter shock. Oh god. Have I completely fucked everything up? I was so deliriously happy when I got the news about the squad, and then he went and called me 'baby,' and it was like all my dreams were coming true at once. Something in me snapped, and then I was just reaching out for the other thing I knew was going to bring me insane amounts of joy.

Or at least in that moment I hoped it would. Right now, he's soaking wet and looking at me with something akin to panic.

"I'm sorry," I rasp. "I didn't mean to pull you in. I was just so excited, and then—"

Nim lunges for me.

Despite being in the chilly pool, I melt as his big hands slip on either side of my neck, and he kisses me with such desperation it's almost frightening. I jump up and wrap my legs around his waist, clinging to his shoulders. But that seems to break the spell, and he snaps his head back, looking concerned.

This time, he's the one to utter, "I'm sorry."

"Don't you dare fucking apologize," I growl, digging my fingers into his biceps and glaring at him. "I wanted you since the moment I saw you."

It's like I can see him working out the math behind his eyes. I nod and, just in case he *still* might not be getting the message, I roll my cock against his stomach. The fact that it's so hard in this cold water should hopefully clear a couple of things up for him.

It does.

He attacks me once again, his kisses like fire. I love that his beard is long enough that it's soft against my skin and smells like the sandalwood oil he uses on it. His arms wrap around my back in a crushing hug, making me feel so safe and secure I could almost cry.

If I weren't so distracted by horniness, that is. I can't believe this is really happening. I'd nearly convinced myself that he wasn't interested, after all. He's given me so many mixed messages over the past couple of weeks. But his signal is coming through loud and clear now.

"Fuck," I mumble into his mouth as I grind against him. "Yes, oh my god, Nim."

"Kitten," he moans back, and *wow*. Something breaks in me in the best possible way. He really just called me that? I don't know whether to melt some more or explode.

As he reaches between us and slips his hand underneath my waterlogged underwear, I lean toward the latter.

"Oh, fuck, *fuck*," I wail, thrusting against his touch.

I'm not just letting go of all this pent-up sexual energy but also the tension from tryouts. It takes an embarrassingly short amount of time before I'm jerking against him and spilling my load as I tremble and my vision blurs.

"That's it, good boy," he murmurs against my ear, and his

words make me feel so gooey I could come all over again. Instead, I shake against him, gasping for air.

Suddenly, I come back to my senses, unlock my legs from around his waist, and drop back down to my feet as the water rushes around us.

Then I lunge for his jeans, wrestling with the wet material to get my hands on his cock. He's looked after me in a million ways, and not just in the orgasm he bestowed on me seconds ago. I desperately want to give him something back. Words are not his strong suit. Perhaps I can take a leaf out of his book and convince him how I feel with my actions instead.

If we weren't in the creek, I'd have sank to my knees to suck him off. Instead, I hastily wrap my fingers around his shaft and start to pump while leaning up to kiss him filthily. His hands are splayed across my back, holding me in place, still taking care of me, even as I try to worship him.

"Good boy," he tells me again, the words rumbling from his mouth straight into mine. "Good kitty."

Fuck, fuck, *fuck*. I don't quite understand what's going on, but it's the hottest thing I've ever experienced in my life. Apparently, he's also pretty damn turned on because it only takes a minute or so before he shudders and clenches his jaw before dropping his head, burying his face against my neck, and moaning.

For a while, we just cling to each other until I start properly shivering. "We need to get out of here," Nim says.

"I don't want this to end," I blurt out before I can even think about playing it cool.

But rather than look weirdly at me, Nim hugs me tighter. "It's not, sweetheart. But I need to get you warm."

Now *that* I can get on board with.

I lean back to look in his eyes, making sure we're on the same wavelength. All I see is that same affection that's been there since he brought me home, except now it's ten times more intense.

Unfortunately, our lovely moment is shattered by a very loud dog bark. We snap our heads around to see a black Labrador come bounding through the foliage, barking again at us in excitement. It gives us just enough time to separate before the dog's owner comes walking out behind them.

She stops when she sees us and raises her eyebrows in concern. I'm hoping the moving water hides our exposed bits and pieces, but I'm still naked aside from my underwear, so I crouch down so at least my nipples are covered. I offer the dog walker a sheepish laugh.

"Fell in," Nim grunts, but his smug grin is possibly a tell. I'm sure that lady knows precisely what we were up to before she arrived, especially after she smiles herself and shakes her head as she walks away.

I can't really bring myself to care. I'm floating on cloud nine.

———

It's a pretty soggy drive back on the bike. I cling to Nim, sharing body heat, so it could have been worse. My clothes might have been mostly dry to start with as I took them off before jumping in, but my body wasn't, and Nim was drenched from head to toe. So by the time we reach the apartment, everything needs peeling off.

During the short journey I'm worried that Nim is going to have changed his mind and want to back off. But as soon as the door is closed, he steps right up into my personal space and rests his hands on my shoulders.

"May I?" he asks.

I'm trembling, feeling his soft breath on my cool skin. It's not helping my brain to do its job, especially when I can't drag my eyes away from his plump, wet lips.

"Uhh…may you what?"

He chuckles, but it's not unkind in any way. If anything, it's fond. Affectionate. "May I get you out of these wet clothes and take care of you, kitten?"

There's that word again, turning my mind into scrambled eggs. "I…I'd like that," I say breathlessly.

If I thought I was shaky before, it's nothing compared to when he starts trailing kisses along my jawline as he slips the leather jacket off me, and drops it to the floor. I moan and tremble, my knees feeling like Jell-O.

"Do you like being called kitten?" he asks.

Immediately, I blush and squirm, like he's discovered my secret. Which is ridiculous because he's the one calling me it. "Um, yeah," I confess. "Is that weird?"

He chuckles and nips at my earlobe. "No. I like kittens."

"You…do?" I say, not quite sure I'm following. "Of course you do. You run a cat café."

He's peeling me out of my hoodie. I've never been undressed by anyone before. It's wildly intimate. I'm resisting the urge to giggle from nerves and sheer overwhelm.

"Yes," he says. "I like those cats a lot. I also like men who wear ears and tails and chase balls of yarn around."

I stare at him, not sure if he's mocking me. It doesn't feel like he is.

I know full well that lots of people love to dress up like cats. Not just as a costume thing but a personality thing. It made me relieved to know that I wasn't alone in feeling that way. But it never really occurred to me that would be something *other people* were attracted to. I thought it was something I had to hide away.

Until I met Nim, that is.

"Really?" I say, watching him crouch down to undo my sneakers.

"Yes," he says simply.

I frown and take a moment to think about that. "You like men cats…and I'm a man cat…and we just happened to meet each other?"

He grunts and flicks his gaze up at me to let me know that this coincidence has not escaped his notice, either. My heart is banging fast, thinking about how he encouraged me to be free and wear my little ears and stuff.

Suddenly, it makes a whole lot of sense how he's basically been hiding from me.

"Nim?" I ask softly as he stands again. We look into each other's eyes. "Is this okay? I wasn't trying to tease you with my clothes or anything, I promise. But I do really like you so much. You're kind and thoughtful and, um, like, really, seriously hot." He huffs out a laugh, and that helps me relax. "I've never told anyone about the cat thing before. Is it really something you've done with other people?"

He nods and gently runs his hands up and down my bare arms. "Yeah," he says. "I have. And you weren't teasing. And… yeah. This is okay. It's what I want. If it's what you want."

"I really, *really,* want it," I say. "But you've got reservations, I can tell."

He clenches his jaw and looks down at my collarbones. "You're young—"

"Not that young," I interject hotly. His mouth twitches with a smile, but I'm serious. That's not an excuse not to pursue this.

"You're my tenant," he tries.

"That just makes it much easier to see each other," I counter. "No schlepping across town between apartments."

He rolls his eyes, but I'm sure I'm amusing him. "We just met," is his next feeble argument.

"People sleep together on first dates. Hell, people meet specifically to have sex and then go on to have relationships after that."

He takes a deep breath, then finally looks at me again. "I don't do hook-ups. I do relationships. My last one ended badly. I wasn't a very good…partner."

"Bullshit," I snap. "You've been amazing to me, and we haven't even been dating."

He chews his lip and considers me. "Thank you. But if we try a relationship…that means a specific sort of thing to me. A lifestyle."

I frown, not quite following. "You mean like living together? We're already doing that."

He shakes his head. "You know how you like being called kitten?"

I rest my hands on his chest, feeling the damp material of his Henley. "I had no idea before today how that would make me feel. It's…like I become someone else when you call me that. And, um, I like being called a good boy, too."

I blush and duck my head, feeling raw and exposed. But he gently touches his thumb to my chin and encourages me to meet his gaze again. "That's part of what I love," he tells me, his voice a low rumble that gives me shivers. "I want you to be my kitten and let me take care of you."

"Like you have been?"

He lifts one shoulder. "And more," he admits. That sends butterflies to my belly. *More?* "I'd also like you to call me something special as well."

I nod eagerly. If there's something that makes him feel how I do when he calls me kitten, I'll do it in a heartbeat.

"I like being called Daddy," he says quietly.

Heat rushes through me. Of course I've heard of Daddies and such, but I've never really thought about how that makes me feel.

Nim wants to take care of me. It's not just what I wanted from Parker, but so much more already, and he says he's not even doing it as much as he'd like yet. When he makes me dinner and drapes blankets over me, it's like I float off and all my troubles melt away. It's kind of how I feel when I'm in full cat mode and…

Ohh…

Okay. Things are starting to make a bit more sense now. I think all these feelings are kind of interconnected.

This is what Nim wants from a relationship with me. Hell, the fact that he wants a relationship at all is kind of mind-blowing to me. After Parker made me feel so utterly disposable, I thought I was done with men for a long time.

But Nim is offering me something so beautiful and pure I'm practically trembling at the thought of it.

And you know, hot. Really hot. I am not some saint over here. I want a big, strong man to take care of me in *every* way.

Does that mean I want a Daddy?

Does it mean I want Nim to be my Daddy?

I lean in and brush my lips over his. "Call me kitten again," I murmur.

"Kitten," he says obediently, kissing me softly.

"Daddy," I say back, trying it out.

God, it feels so good, so fucking *right*.

In a flash, his mouth is devouring mine, and I'm enveloped by his arms. In that moment I sense that despite both our hesitations, this is it. We're all in now. What I'm feeling is so strong it feels foolish to try and fight it, anyway. I'm caught in the hurricane, and I don't even want to try and get free.

I've been swept up in this madness, and that's okay with me.

"Need to get you warm, kitten," he mumbles between kisses.

"Yes, Daddy," I say, getting more confident.

He groans and before I can blink, he's picked me up in his arms like I weigh nothing. I've still got my jeans on, and he's fully clothed, but we're not dripping as much as before as we move through the apartment.

I wish yet again that I'd been conscious that first night when he took me from the sofa to my bed. But now I realize this could be a thing that happens regularly, and my cock is very, very interested in this idea.

"Oh my god," I say with a giggle, clinging to him and burying my face against his neck.

"Good kitten," he says as he walks us to the bathroom.

Something comes over me in a rush. I'm not sure what it is, but it's like a dizzy mix of daring but also a calm conviction.

I meow against his skin.

He stops in his tracks, and I move my head slightly so we can look at each other. He's got an almost wondrous expression on his face.

"*Good* kitty," he says before nuzzling his nose against my cheek.

He takes great care in stripping me all the way naked. It gives me shivers letting him do that. But I'm soon distracted as I finally get to see him naked, and all my daydreams were pretty damned accurate. There are even more tattoos, his chest is lovely and hairy, and his cock is thick and strong looking.

I'm in heaven.

I showered plenty of times with Parker, but that either involved us having sex or getting cleaned after sex. I always took care of myself. However, when I reach for the shampoo in Nim's bathroom, he bats my hand down.

"Bad kitty," he says with a smirk. It makes my insides all warm.

At first, I feel a little awkward just standing there and letting him wash my hair and body. But eventually, I start to relax, swaying as his hands work all over me. It gives me a chance to admire the view.

He's got a magnificent body. Very different to mine, but that's a good thing. He's so broad and much hairier than me. I can tell he's strong and obviously muscular. He's got some great man boobs going on. But there's a softer layer on top too that makes him cuddly.

And the tattoos, jeez. From the wings across his clavicles to the roses and skulls down his arms, I just want to inspect every single one of them and hear the story behind them. He really is beautiful.

From the way his fingers are exploring me, I'd say he's equally fascinated. He *loves* rubbing his thumbs over my pierced nipples as he kisses me, and I have to admit I'm a big fan of that as well. He's soon got one hand wrapped around both of our cocks, stroking them together leisurely.

"Daddy," I whimper, knowing it'll affect us both.

Sure enough, he groans and picks up the pace, our kisses getting messier. "My little kitten," he says.

The idea of belonging to him, of being his, tips me over the edge. I cry out as I come, digging my fingers into his arms to stop my knees from buckling. When I catch my breath and see he's still hard, I do what I wanted to do in the creek and drop to my knees, beyond eager to swallow him down. He grunts and strokes my hair, looking down on me as I look up at him through my eyelashes, the water falling all around us.

He comes, and I drink it down like milk. As soon as he's recovered his senses, he helps me to stand, wraps me in his arms, and kisses the top of my head.

"Mine," he growls. "My kitty."

"Yes, Daddy," I agree.

I had no idea how today was going to pan out. I never would have believed in a million years that I'd actually end up having sex *twice* with the man I've been falling for or that night I'd be sleeping in his bed. In some ways, I can acknowledge that this has all happened pretty fast.

But on the other hand, it's the most natural thing that I've ever experienced. So why should I fight it?

For once, this little kitty seems to have fallen on his feet, right into the lap of a perfect Daddy. *And* I made the competition squad.

Nothing's going to stop me now.

CHAPTER 13

Nim

"OKAY. COME ON. SPILL."

I quickly school my features like I wasn't just smiling into the dishwasher as I was loading it. Clearing my throat, I turn around and arch an eyebrow at Leah. "What?"

She wags a finger at me. "Don't you give me that nonsense," she warns. "You're drifting through the day like angels are fluttering around your head, playing their tiny little harps in a tune only you can hear. Something happened with the cute kitty boy, didn't it? I want details. All of them. And so help you if you skip the good parts."

I clench my jaw and try not to react, but the smile creeps onto my face anyway.

"I *knew* it!" she shrieks, causing several people to look our way. The little tabby kitten appears from nowhere and scales my leg so he can perch on my shoulder like my miniature bodyguard. Unfortunately, nothing is going to deter Leah from her questioning.

I shrug. "Yeah," I say before sidestepping her to serve a customer.

We have one of the other guys behind the counter with

us, so no one is getting neglected. And for some unknown reason, it's strangely quiet in here today. We had a few canceled bookings, and walk-ins are about half what they usually are. I'm hoping it's just a weird glitch. Business naturally ebbs and flows, after all.

But Leah is frighteningly good at multitasking. She can brew coffee and interrogate all at the same time.

"That's not 'details,' Benjamin," she scoffs. "Is it serious? Are you going to put a little collar and bell on him?"

I roll my eyes but honestly, I'm bursting with so much happiness I actually feel like telling her just a little. I lean closer and give her a meaningful look. "He's mine," I say simply.

She genuinely swoons.

"Oh. My. *God*. I knew it. This is amazing!"

"Excuse me?"

I look up expecting to see someone impatiently waiting to be served. Instead, I'm met with a pale face, piercing blue eyes, and long black hair. The woman's slender hands are loosely clasped in front of her chest, her nails as black as the corset and blouse she's wearing. Atop her head is a delicate, dark blue flower crown. Rather than looking hurried or annoyed, she's studying me curiously.

"Hi," I say, glancing at Leah. Her mouth is slightly hanging open, though, and she's frozen in her tracks. I get the feeling that I'm going to have to handle this particular customer by myself. "Can I help you?"

The dark-haired woman narrows her eyes at the tabby on my shoulder before looking around the rest of the café. "Where's the new one?"

"New...what?"

"Cat," she elaborates. "A black one."

I shake my head. "We haven't had any new cats join us for a while, I'm afraid." My heart skips a beat. I'd know if there had been any black cats because I'd have already started worrying how I was going to take on *another* one if they got left here for too long like the others.

She frowns and looks back at me. "The tea leaves were very clear," she says.

I blink. "Um…sorry?" I offer her.

She opens her mouth as if to speak. But then her eyes widen, suddenly turning her head toward the door. "Blessed be," she mutters. "Stand your ground."

Before I can respond, she sweeps away in a flurry of layered black skirts that rustle and boots that must have reinforced heels to tap on the tiles like they do. She whirls into an empty seat that just happened to be available at a nearby table. We never have empty seats. That's kind of our thing.

I go to open my mouth and ask her what she's talking about when the bell above the door tinkles, and three people come striding in. Their appearance finally seems to snap Leah out of her trance as she jumps to attention. "Oh what fresh hell is this," she mutters, dashing to my side.

Leading the party is the prim and proper blonde woman with crimson nails who came in the other day. Today, she's wearing a skintight light blue pencil dress with a little white jacket and more clippy-cloppy heels. Her smile is bright, but it doesn't reach her eyes, which are homing in on me as she approaches.

Behind her is a weasel-like man with a thin mustache and greasy hair parted in the middle, wearing a beige jacket and clutching a digital camera with a big flash like you might see in the hands of a member of the paparazzi.

Bringing up the rear is a very pissed-off-looking Sheriff Chancey, hands on her hips, ignoring everyone in the café who has paused in what they're doing to watch this mini-parade. She's also only got eyes for me.

"I'm so sorry about this, Nim," she begins to say. But Blondie has stopped in front of me. She opens up the clasp to her purse, thrusting her hand inside, her red nails flashing as she withdraws an envelope.

"Good afternoon, Mr. Decker," she says with a cheeriness that I don't buy for a second. "Allow me to introduce myself. I'm Mrs. Durham and this is my associate, Mr. Humphrey, from the County Office of Environmental Health. I'm afraid there have been some complaints."

"Complaints?" I repeat, bewildered.

"Hang on," Leah pipes up. "Mrs. Durham? As in the mayor's wife?"

When it becomes clear that I'm not going to take the stupid bit of paper, Mrs. Durham places it smoothly down on the counter, her cold smile not faltering. "I am merely here as a concerned member of the public," she tells Leah, her words dripping with fake sincerity.

"So it's you who complained," I say through gritted teeth, crossing my arms and scowling at her. She was annoying when she came in here before, but I didn't think she was actually anything to worry about.

She gives me a dainty shrug, pressing her hands together. "Complaints were made. That's all I can say."

"About what?" Leah snaps.

"Hygiene, of course," Mrs. Durham says with a chuckle, flicking her fingers to encompass the room. "Is this an eatery or a petting zoo? It's very concerning."

"As we said before," Leah counters hotly, "we have all the correct licensing and pass regular inspections."

Mrs. Durham sniffs and looks back at me. "I'm sure that's all fine, but Mr. Humphrey is here nonetheless to take photographs, food samples, and copies of your records. Then the board of inspectors will decide."

"On what?" I ask.

Fear is bubbling inside me, but it's being overshadowed by anger. Let this woman just try and come for me. My establishment is spotless, but more importantly, it's essential for hundreds of cats getting adopted all over the local area.

"Whether it's safe for you to keep serving customers," Mrs. Durham says, fluttering her eyelashes. "We have to make sure everything's above board. There are children here, after all." She turns and beams at the first little girl she lays her eyes on. "We don't want you getting sick, now do we, dear?"

The child's lip wobbles. There's a gray cat currently sitting at the table with her and her parents. The girl throws her arms around the unsuspecting feline and hugs him to her chest. "Don't hurt Mr. Truffles!" she cries before bursting into tears.

Mrs. Durham blinks and steps back in shock.

"There's nothing wrong with Toe Beans," a young man in a Panthers letter jacket says. He's sitting with a pretty girl who nods emphatically as he crosses his arms and glares at the blonde woman. "What are you causing trouble for?"

"I have to agree," another man from the line says with a posh English accent. "This is highly unnecessary." I recognize him because he's one of those environmental types who always bring their own reusable cup in. I wish more people did that. In fact, I even knock off a quarter for those that do to try and encourage it.

Mrs. Durham is still smiling, but her lips are pinched as she turns back to us. "Well. Let's get on with it, shall we? I assume we are free to go wherever we need to, Mr. Decker."

I grunt at her. "Office is locked."

"Perhaps you can find the keys so we can access it, then. Hmm?"

I grunt again. Fine. But if I'm letting them in to snoop over my files, I'm watching every single thing they do.

"Goodness me, look at the time," the dark-haired woman says, rising to her feet like a specter.

I'd forgotten she was watching. Mrs. Durham ignores her, but Leah's head immediately snaps back to look at her, biting her lip like she's nervous. I'm not sure what that's about, but I'm more interested as the pale woman flips a very small doll between her spindly fingers, deftly dropping it into Mrs. Durham's open purse without the other woman noticing.

Before I can be sure I saw what I really saw, the mysterious woman looks at me again. "When you need me, come find me. I'll be waiting." Her gaze shifts to Leah, who squirms at her attention. "Blessed be."

She sweeps outside into the sunshine like a storm cloud carried on a zephyr.

Mrs. Durham huffs, all pretenses of her smile gone. "Right, well, if everyone is quite done, I think we should begin our work. Mr. Humphrey?"

"Certainly, madame," he says sleazily.

I don't relish them poking about my beloved café, but there doesn't seem to be much I can do to stop them. Sheriff Chancey throws her hands up as the other two move to the back of the café. "It's out of my hands," she hisses, clearly mad as a snake. "I think it's best just to let them get on with it."

"What the hell is going on?" Leah demands in a low voice as the café starts to return to normal. People talk among themselves. My other staff begin serving waiting customers. The little girl lets go of Mr. Truffles, and he immediately runs to go hide atop one of the cat trees.

Chancey shakes her head and leans on the counter. "I don't know but I also don't think it's anything good. We had reports that stolen cars were being moved through Horowitz's garage and that the Butterflies nail salon was employing illegal immigrants. It all turned out to be horseshit, but…"

"But all those businesses are run by members of the Cardinals," I say, my heart dropping. "Or at least employ them. First O'Toole's, now this?"

Chancey sighs, giving me a pitying look. "You heard there were rumors that Mayor Durham was being investigated for embezzlement, right?"

Leah and I share a glance. "No," I say.

"Exactly," Chancey replies. "No one has. Because he's gone on this rampage to clean up a town with very little crime in an attempt to distract everyone from what's really going on and keep their attention away from his opponent, Mr. Sanchez. He's giving voters a villain who he can conveniently defeat in the run up to the election."

"My family?" I ask.

"A violent biker gang," she counters. "People don't care about the truth. They're happy to lean into old stereotypes, especially when respectable ladies start getting hysterical about children's safety. I tell you—they'll be coming for the school's Dungeons & Dragons club next."

She's distracted as the tiny tabby kitten takes a flying leap from my shoulder onto the counter where she's been leaning during her rant. The fluffy baby skitters to a halt, then starts happily stomping up the sleeve of her uniform.

"Well, hello there!" she says in delight. "It's my friend from the pub! How are you, little darling?"

I'm glad to have a moment to think as Chancey is charmed by the kitten. I watch Durham and Humphrey skulk around my beloved café, taking photos of my fur babies and getting in the faces of my patrons.

"Urgh, karma is *so* coming for them," Leah mumbles as she folds her arms and glares.

Is that why business has been down for a few days? Has this harpy been scaring people off and telling people lies about my business practices?

Well, they can try all they like. I know that Toe Beans has never put a foot wrong or failed any inspection in all the years it's been running.

But if the mayor's wife starts a smear campaign, it's going to be hard to battle that.

Unless we fight fire with fire.

"Leah," I say. She's staring daggers at our two intruders as well, but she turns to me at the sound of her name. "You make any TikToks lately? Or Instagrams?"

It takes her a second to catch on. Usually, she'd give me hell for calling those things the wrong words, but not today. Today, a devilish grin spreads on her face. "You mean like a quick 'day in the life' sort of thing about all our amazing health and safety regulations with some cute kitty co-stars?"

I shrug nonchalantly despite feeling a small rush of satisfaction. We've got something like fifty thousand followers on each platform who adore us. Leah even set up a merchandise shop that brings in a surprising amount of income each month.

I imagine they'd have a lot to say about our mayor and his bogus accusations if they found out.

"Only if you have the time," I say, catching Chancey's eye. The sheriff winks at me.

"I'll go get my phone," Leah says, already rushing off.

I exhale and rub the back of my neck. Don't get me wrong. I'm more than willing to fight for my home and my family. But it's hard to ignore the uneasiness that's settled in my stomach. In these kinds of battles, it rarely goes well for the misfit outcasts.

It's even harder knowing that I'm not just fighting for myself.

I look around at all the cats that live here, hoping one day to be adopted. If we have to close, they'll be forced to go back to the shelter, where their chances will be much lower of finding their forever homes. Then there's my staff that obviously have bills to pay.

And then there's Jessie.

I have only just promised him that I am going to take care of him. This relationship is still brand new and delicate. He's relying on me. I can't let him down. I've got a second chance at being someone's Daddy with someone I care deeply for.

This bullshit health inspection could completely ruin everything. That feeling of being out of control is sneaking back into my chest, and I hate it. After my biological family disowned me, I swore that no one would ever make me feel this way again. But if the mayor is determined to make the Cardinals his scapegoat, there might be only so much we can do to fight that.

But I will fight. For me and everyone I love. No way am I making it easy for the Durhams. This is my town. My family. My cats. My kitten.

I protect what's mine.

CHAPTER 14

Jessie

SO MUCH FOR SWEARING OFF MEN FOR THE FORESEEABLE future.

I have to laugh at myself because I'm not even mad about it. Not when I'm sleeping in Nim's bed every night now and he looks at me with cartoon heart eyes every time he thinks I'm not paying attention.

He's still not very good with words. In fact, over the past few days he's been even *more* quiet than usual. I've asked him a couple of times what's wrong, but he just shrugs, smiles, then distracts me with delicious kisses that I'm powerless to resist. I'm sure something's going on, and after the bullshit lies Parker fooled me with, I'm a tiny bit nervous. But Nim isn't Parker, that's for sure. I try and trust that when he's ready, he'll tell me. And until then, I do my best to assure myself that it's not anything to do with us.

I didn't realize how much anxiety I'd been carrying around regarding how unimportant Parker made me feel. I didn't have another serious boyfriend to compare it to, so I figured that's just how busy adults had relationships.

Bullshit.

Even if Nim is tired or stressed or preoccupied, he always finds ways to make me feel important. He doesn't need words when he's always making me meals, massaging my shoulders, or stopping me before I run out of the door to press a sweet kiss to my cheek.

I kind of wish we'd met over the summer. I know he has to work most days, but that's the beauty of him living above the café. His commute is a matter of minutes, and I can always swing by and say hello when I'm coming and going between classes.

Since I started college, though, my schedule has been hectic in addition to the few short shifts I'm working for him. Plus, the Kittens have regular football and basketball games to attend. We're also working toward the Snowdown competition in Chicago before Christmas that doesn't just involve training but fundraising as well. I never stop. My head is spinning so much I find it hard to fall asleep at night.

Well, until Nim tires me out, that is.

He's been quite firm about taking it slow in that department. We haven't gone further than hand and blow jobs. And that's *fine.* I am still having plenty of fun. I just worry sometimes he thinks I'm not ready when I am. If I have to prove that to him and earn his trust, that's okay. I do like the idea that he's in this for the long run.

In the meantime, he's been playing some games with me. Not sexy games—not really. At first, I wasn't sure. But he says I can do more than just wear my kitten stuff. That I can get into what he calls a 'headspace' as well. That was when he sat on the bed and produced a ball of yarn.

I felt self-conscious and silly to begin with as I knelt on the floor and watched him jerking the colorful thread around. But almost immediately his actual cats started stalking it, wiggling their butts before they pounced. Nim smiled and laughed with such delight at their antics it made me brave enough to try it as well. I wanted to make him feel like that, too.

When I tried my first wiggle and pounded, he cried out in happy surprise, calling me a good kitty. The more I played, the lighter I became. It was amazing.

Since then, we've had a couple of sessions with a bouncy ball and a laser pointer. I would have been worried that it was boring for him, but every time he gets so happy and animated seeing me play. It's a lot to wrap my head around, but he genuinely seems to get as much of a kick out of it as I do.

Then there's the grooming. Now that *is* sexy. He gets me to lie across his lap on the bed while he brushes my hair. Usually, I just wear a pair of soft shorts with my ears and paws. Because then he has this fine-toothed metal comb that he drags across my bare skin that I adore. It gives me shivers just thinking about it. By the time he's done I'm always so blissed out and turned on that when he inevitably wraps his lips around my hard cock, I come within about thirty seconds before passing out.

He never minds. I always wake up later, all tucked up in bed, usually with him curled up beside me.

So, yeah, I might be craving a thorough pounding from my big strong man, but I can't for one second claim I'm being neglected, and I wouldn't want to. I guess I'm still just a bit insecure that what we're doing is enough. That is probably insane because all I wanted from Parker was for him to dote on me. Now I have a partner who's doing just that and I'm worried that I'm being selfish or that I'm not worth it.

Honestly, I eye roll at myself so hard sometimes.

I think it might be easier if I could muster up the courage to ask him what this is, officially. I never did that with Parker. I made assumptions, and that backfired spectacularly. I want to ask Nim if we're exclusive. If I'm his boyfriend, not just his kitten. That's such a private thing for us, after all. Would he want to be public with me like Parker never was?

The trouble is that words are so difficult for him. I feel like he needs to be in just the right frame of mind before I try and bring this up. Otherwise, he might clam up and run away, hiding his thoughts from me. But if the relationship has moved on further—if it's stronger—that might make us both feel more mature.

I don't know.

But that's probably why I find myself detouring to the library after class on a whim one afternoon. It's usually pretty quiet whenever I've been in there to check out books. Possibly because the librarian is such an intimidating woman that I've seen members of the football team jump into bushes in order to avoid her. Maybe I'm biased, since she generally has a black cat glued to her ankles wherever she goes, but her goth clothes and piercing stare don't really scare me.

The thought of not being a good enough kitten for Nim when he's given me so much makes me feel sick, however. So does the thought of him catching me doing any sort of research. I know he knows I'm inexperienced, but I don't want him to actually know how clueless I am, you know? It's embarrassing.

Hence why I'd rather find a secluded corner of the college library and see what I can learn by myself. I know Nim wants to go slowly as I'm only just discovering my inner kitten. But I want to surprise him.

It's me who gets a shock, however, just as I'm approaching the library doors. I'd heard that there was a raccoon that lives on campus and is almost treated like a bit of a mascot or pet by a lot of the students. But until now, I'd only seen Clayton from afar.

When he runs in front of me with an honest-to-god box of cupcakes in his little paws, I almost trip over myself as I jump out of my skin. It's just not something I'd been expecting to see as I crossed the courtyard.

As he disappears into the foliage, I look around. However, no one is chasing him, shaking their fist, and yelling "Thief!" I decide that he's obviously worked hard for it, so why shouldn't he get to keep his prize? Good for him, I say.

Idly, I wonder if there are people out there who pet play as raccoons. There probably are. If people like being puppies, dragons, horses, and bunnies, why not raccoons? It would be pretty easy to get an adorable little eye mask to mimic the markings.

That brings me back to my task at hand. Scanning the desks once I'm inside, I see that there's that same young Hispanic guy with glasses who always seems to be at the table by the fire escape. Sometimes he's alone or sometimes he seems to be tutoring other students, which seems odd given his age, but whatever. I need privacy, so I move away from them and find a desk by the window. Unless someone comes right up to the glass, they won't be able to see my screen.

Perfect.

I get my headphones out. It brings me a lot of joy, knowing that Nim loves the ears on them as much as I do. Putting them on, I feel calmer displaying a bit of myself on the outside. It doesn't matter if no one realizes what it really means. I do and that's enough. I put on a playlist I made that's more synth wave and vibes than lyrics. I want the music to wash over me, not distract me.

Taking a few deep breaths, I rub the back of my hand against my cheek, letting my kitten come more to the surface as I start my internet search. I've been on a million sites regarding kitty aesthetics, but I never bothered to look too much into the psychology of it.

I open up a few tabs, typing in things like 'What is kitten

play?' and 'How to be a good kitten.' I'm soon completely lost in various pages that give me a whole load of advice.

I've done a lot of head nuzzles and meows since we started playing, but the internet is suggesting I could be doing more in terms of pawing to get what I want. Even biting. I don't like the idea of trying to hurt Nim, but then I think about how the likes of Libra will often press her teeth against my arm or hand. But rather than bite, she'll just rest her teeth there, looking up at me to ensure she's caught my attention.

I could do that.

It's crazy how my heart starts thumping in my chest the more I read. It gives me ideas like making a little cozy bed on the floor made of blankets I can knead. My nails aren't great from how much I bite them, so maybe I could try using the real cats' scratching posts. That sounds like it might hurt my fingertips, though, so I'm not sure.

One thing I *definitely* want to try is eating from a bowl on the floor or sitting at Nim's feet and having him give me treats. I don't entirely understand why, but the idea of those things makes me feel extremely swoony. I hope Nim might be interested in something like that.

My giddiness is probably what emboldens me to open up a new search I promised I wouldn't look for until I'd locked myself in a bathroom or something. But I'm saturated with all these lovely kitten ideas, and now I want to investigate further.

Into a tail.

Not the kind I clip to my clothes. I know how much Nim loves that already, and obviously it's given me a lot of joy before I even met him.

It's time to take it to the next level.

My heart is in my throat as I begin to look through the various search results I get from looking for tails attached to butt plugs. I've never put anything like that inside myself before. I've played with dildos, but they didn't do too much for me, so I mostly stuck to jerking off if I couldn't get an actual dick. For the last few years, that was just Parker, and in retrospect, his was pretty disappointing.

The sheer number of options coming up on my screen is kind of overwhelming. There are lots of cheap options, but I don't know if cheap is better in this instance. I'm also a bit confused between silicone versus metal. They both seem to have pros and cons. Then there are the designs themselves in every color I can think of. Some have matching ears. But I have ears already. Is it extravagant to think about getting another pair? What if—

A hand waves in front of my face.

My heart almost stops.

I snatch my headphones off, slam the laptop down, and stare in horror at the stranger grinning at me. He holds up his hands. "Whoa there, kitty!" he whispers and winks at me.

My heart is racing as my gaze skitters over him. He's got a stunning mop of sandy blond curls with golden highlights, sparkling blue eyes, and a neatly trimmed five o'clock shadow. A single pearl earring shaped like a teardrop dangles from his left earlobe, and he's wearing a black lacy shirt.

Okay…so not some homophobic jock about to kick my ass, I assume.

"What…uh…" I stammer.

He chuckles and sits in the chair beside me. "Sorry. I didn't mean to scare you. I did say hello and wave, but you were pretty engrossed. I couldn't help but notice the interesting subject you're researching."

He waggles his eyebrows as I blush furiously and wish the ground would swallow me up.

"You shouldn't be snooping on people," I mumble, crossing my arms and shrinking down in my chair.

Rather than take offense, he laughs softly again. "Girl, you shouldn't be in a public library if you don't want someone 'accidentally' seeing what you're up to." He uses air quotes and I'm almost certain that there was nothing accidental in him coming over here.

"I'm sorry if I offended you," I say, still feeling thoroughly mortified.

He huffs out a scornful little laugh and nods. "Yeah, you should be sorry. Give me that."

Before I can stop him, he's opened up my laptop again. I obviously hadn't closed it all the way as the screen hasn't locked. So there my search results are in all their butt plug glory.

Kill me now.

He tuts and starts typing. "You shouldn't go to big soul-less companies for this sort of thing. Here. My friend makes unique handmade pieces. Better to support self-employed queer creatives rather than some CEO who's only interested in exploiting the LGBT community for profit, right?"

I blink at the stranger as he turns my laptop back toward me. He's brought up a website, this specific page dedicated to kitten accessories. The prices are mid-range, but the colors and designs are exquisite. I stare at the screen for a second before looking back at him.

"Do you often accost random people and suggest fetish wear to them?" I ask, genuinely curious.

He snickers wickedly. It's a delicious sound that sends tingles up my spine, I have to admit. Although I'm not sure I'm really attracted to him, as beautiful as he is. There's something intimidating about him.

"Only ones I can tell are kinky from a mile off," he says proudly, as if daring me to tell me he's wrong.

I don't.

"Well…thank you," I say with a nervous laugh. "These look amazing. I'm Jessie. Are you, um, a kitten as well?"

He shakes his head. "No. But I'm on the scene. I have a different thing. Kadence."

He offers me his hand and I shake it, surprised at how strong his grip is. Yeah, Kadence is a little scary, but I can't help but like him anyway.

He lets me go as he looks me up and down. "I haven't seen you before," he states.

I shake my head. "No, I'm a freshman, but I graduated high school a few years ago."

"Oh," Kadence says with a wave of his hand. "Yeah, we get a lot of that around here. I suppose it's a community college thing. It just makes it easier to have parties when everyone can legally drink. I'm a senior, but I try my best to seek out all the kinksters. My friend Harper is like you. Just started even though he's in his early twenties. You see him over there with one of his Daddies?"

So many of the words he just used pinged in my brain. There are other kinky people in this town? I suppose that's a stupid thing to be surprised by, but it seems so…cute and wholesome, even if it's somewhat dilapidated.

I look over to the check-in desk where Kadence has just indicated. There's a slim blond guy standing beside a stocky Asian man as he talks to the emo librarian. *"One* of his Daddies?" I repeat. "Hang on, that's Coach Ritter from the football team." He's the assistant coach, not the main one, but I've seen him on the sidelines at games.

Kadence flicks his eyebrows at me. "Yeah. Harper has *three* Daddies, and they like to chase him down and fuck him where they catch him. How hot is that?"

I shiver, not really knowing how I feel. It probably is super hot. But it seems a little aggressive for me. I glance back at Kadence and wonder just what kind of kink he's into.

Probably being tied up and whipped and stuff. That seems a little extreme. Or at least it is right now. God, I'm so fucking green.

"Being chased is not my thing," Kadence says with a wink as if reading my mind.

"Oh," I say, embarrassed at being caught out. "Do you, um, have a Daddy, though?"

"Not right now, no," he says with a shrug. "I like to have a charcuterie board of lovers, you know? At the moment, I'm seeing this absolute fuck boi who's so far in the closet I swear he's looking for Narnia. It's almost certainly going to end in tears, but right now, the sneaking around is exhilarating."

He shimmies his shoulders and grins at me, and I can't help but laugh. "If you say so."

"Aww, Jessie," he says and bumps my shoulder. "Sorry, I didn't mean to scare you. You're a baby kitty, aren't you?" I blush and look at him through my eyelashes, but he gives me a fond look. "And does that mean you have a new Daddy you want to impress?"

I probably get stars in my eyes, but I don't care. "Yeah," I say dreamily as I think about Nim. "He's so kind and generous and hot and, um…"

Kadence flicks his eyes toward the screen. "And you want to get a special present for him, huh? Why don't you let your new auntie Kiki help you pick out something perfect?" He leans closer. "That's me, by the way."

I laugh and look at him curiously. "You really do want to be friends with a random stranger you just met in the library," I marvel.

He pokes out his tongue, like he's going to touch the tip of his nose, then makes a kissy noise at me. "You're a stray kitty —how could I resist? Besides, I collect kinky little queers like Pokémon. Oh! Do you have Professor Knight?"

"For classics?" I say, confused by the apparent non sequitur.

Kadence nods eagerly. "Rumor has it he's totally fucking his TA from last year. I think the guy still uses he/him pronouns. But all I know is that about halfway through the year, he started wearing tennis skirts and stuff. He really rocked those outfits. I miss looking at his butt in class. But, yes, anyway—the kinksters are everywhere in this naughty little town. Stick with me, and I'll show you the way!"

I'm not entirely sure what to make of this person who has bulldozed his way into my life, but I must admit it will be nice to have friends outside of the cheer squad. I'm still really close with Alannah, but she didn't make the competition team, and I can tell she's trying really hard not to make things awkward, even though she's sad. I'm sad. I have to look at Tara's stupid face all the time instead.

But Kadence could be just the kind of friend I need, especially if he knows much more about the scene than me.

"I'd love some help, thank you," I admit.

We have fun on my laptop for another hour or so, and before we leave, I make sure we swap numbers. I head home filled with tantalizing excitement, imagining the look on Nim's face when he sees my surprise for him.

I'm going to be the best kitten he's ever met. After I'm through with him, he'll realize just what an amazing Daddy he truly is.

And maybe that will be enough to label this thing officially.

CHAPTER 15

Nim

"SEE WHAT I MEAN?" DONNA SAYS GLUMLY AS I WALK UP TO O'Toole's. She's come to meet me in the parking lot, her arms folded and a grim look on her face.

Probably because there's a crowd of about twenty people outside of her pub, all holding signs and shouting nonsense. I pick up phrases like "Not in our town!" and "Think of the children!"

"What the fuck?" I grunt, genuinely not sure I can believe my eyes. Don't these people have anything better to do?

Apparently not. I'm not sure if members of this crowd know Mayor Durham personally or if he's just managed to whip up this many voters into such an organic frenzy. The result is the same.

I know my business is down, and I don't have a mob actively trying to dissuade people from going inside.

Yet.

"Have you called Sheriff Chancey?" I ask.

Donna shrugs as we walk together back toward the front door. "It's free speech and all that, isn't it? If these clowns can terrorize Planned Parenthood without repercussions, there sure as shit isn't a good argument to get them off my property. Technically, if they stay on the public sidewalk, they aren't doing anything wrong." She gives me a sly look. "I might have thought about turning the water hose on them once or twice."

Honestly, that sounds pretty tempting to me.

"Go back to where you came from!" one pinched-looking man yells at me. "Paddle Creek doesn't want your kind here!"

Even though he's half my size and I'm a full-grown adult now, his words still sting. Some people are so consumed by hate they don't stop to think about what they're actually demanding. Would he still be so righteous if he saw a teenage boy shivering and hungry on the streets? Or if he knew the all-consuming terror of knowing there isn't one single person on earth who gives a damn whether you live or die?

"Excuse me, sir," Donna says cheerfully as we push our way through the crowd. None of them actually touch us, but they get right up in our faces.

"Down with immorality!" another woman cries, shaking her fist. She's holding a sign that reads 'Protect our children!' and I do my best not to snarl. Protect them from what?

"You'd know all about immorality, wouldn't you, Sharron?" Donna quips with a smirk. "Your husband aware you stepped out on him with your gym instructor?"

The woman's face turns purple, and she shuts up long enough for me to follow Donna inside, where there is a distinct lack of drugs or hookers. I breathe a sigh of relief as the familiar smell of worn leather greets us, AC/DC playing on the sound system.

The place is practically empty, though. I wince and glance over at Donna, who throws her hands up and stomps over to the bar. "I know, I know. Don't start," she gripes. "We'll be okay. If we can just make it through this election, hopefully, things will calm down. After Christmas, everyone will have forgotten all about it."

I chew my lip, not so sure. If Durham gets re-elected, is he really going to leave us alone? Or is he going to follow through on his election promises and shut all our businesses down?

Legally, he hasn't got a leg to stand on. It's more the word-of-mouth slander that's killing us slowly. My profits have probably halved in the past week.

Leah's noticed, and I'm sure some of my other staff probably have too. But I'm trying to shield Jessie from it all as best I can.

My heart aches just thinking about him. I still can't believe this is really happening between us. But I worry I'm being selfish in wanting him as much as I do. Surely, he deserves someone better than me with all my problems? He keeps asking me what's wrong but I'm bottling it up. He doesn't need to know that the café and my biker community are both in trouble. He should be focusing on school and the cheer squad, not getting dragged down by my issues.

Part of me knows, however, that me not talking to him *is* the problem. In fact, it's exactly what I fucked up with before when Brent and I were together.

I order a Guinness from Donna. As desperate as I am to get home to Jessie, I need a little time to think. It's enough to be running my own business without fretting about all this crap on top of it. I want to do something for my community, though. We can't let those bastards outside win. We haven't done anything wrong.

If they're trying to intimidate people from coming inside, then we need people who aren't easily intimidated.

"Drag queen," I mumble.

I don't blame Donna as she raises her eyebrows at me. "A

new hobby you're thinking of trying?" she asks with a teasing grin.

I huff but also give her a half smile to let her know I'm aware that she's pulling my leg. "There's that drag queen from Creams. Kimmi Sugar. Ask her to host a charity bingo night or something here. We'll invite local chapters to come."

Donna tilts her head. "Out-of-towners as reinforcements," she says, nodding in approval. "That could work. That could work for everyone. We could encourage them to get their bikes serviced at Horowitz's while they're here."

I hum in agreement. Not that the idea of interacting with a whole load of people fills me with joy. But it's amazing what lengths I'll go to when I feel like my family is in danger.

I take another sip of my drink then leave the rest on the counter. "You'll put the call out?" I ask, rising to head out. As much as I want to give Donna my support, I have a kitten at home that I need to get back to, not to mention actual cats that might need my attention if Jessie hasn't had the chance today. I promised him I wouldn't be late once I'd checked up on the situation here, and I want him to know he can trust me to keep my word.

We've agreed to take it all slow, partly because I'm so afraid that I want *everything* with Jessie. We already live together, though, so I don't want to pressure him too soon into anything he's not ready for. Be that moving his things from his room to mine, escalating our intimacy, or even just labeling what's going on. He calls me Daddy, and I fucking love that. But he might not want to think of me yet as his boyfriend or partner or whatever. Being his Daddy is certainly enough for me. I don't need anything else. So until he pushes it, I don't see the need to rush him.

Try as I might, I can't stop myself from wanting to be near him all the damn time. I'm going to piss him off with my clinginess, I'm sure. But it's as if my body is craving his whenever he's not around. Those people out there think there's a drug problem going on in here? They might be right, just not in the way they expect.

I am fully addicted to Jessie Garras, and I have no idea how to quit.

When I head out, Donna is already going through her phone, presumably reaching out to our wider community for reinforcements. As soon as I walk through the door, the protesters on her doorstep reactivate, yelling at me that I'm what's wrong with this country and how I should be ashamed of myself.

I'd laugh if I weren't so afraid of the damage they could cause.

There's not much I can do tonight. I've already sparked an idea for Donna that might help. So I throw my leg over my bike and head on home. Even just driving through the streets of Paddle Creek helps relax me a bit. This *is* my home, and I'll be damned if anyone is going to take that away from me.

As I come through the apartment door, there's no sign of Jessie. It's after seven, so I would have thought he'd be home. Sometimes I find him cooking for us if he's beaten me to it or maybe studying on the couch. What I find is a lot of sleepy cats and a note in Jessie's pretty handwriting.

Come to the bedroom and shut the door behind you x

My heart rate picks up. We try and keep the fur babies out when we're being intimate as it's just a bit weird otherwise. I won't lie, with all the stress I'm carrying around, I don't need to be asked twice to indulge in a little alone time with my baby boy.

Trying not to rush and disturb my horde of cats, I make my way to the main bedroom as fast as I can, slipping inside without allowing any unwanted guests in behind me.

My first thought is that it's dark in here. The sun might

still be setting outside, but the heavy curtains have been pulled, limiting the late evening sunshine. Several candles have been lit, so I can see that there are a few blankets on the bed. It looks like Jessie has made a cozy little nest for himself.

That's when my eyes fix on him, though, and honestly, the rest of the apartment could catch fire right now, and I wouldn't notice.

My kitten has bought himself some new things.

I freeze on the spot with my jaw hanging open as he stretches out on the mattress. The fluffy ears nestled in his dark hair are a beautiful minty green with light pink on the inside. The paw slippers on his feet and the fingerless gloves on his hands are a matching green, as is the leather harness strapped to his chest. They're all embellished with diamantés that sparkle in the candlelight.

As he rolls on the bed and grins up at me, I can see that he's finished the ensemble with a bright white satin jockstrap that clings sinfully to his junk, showing me every ridge and curve of his cock. But the pièce de résistance is the luxurious fluffy tail that falls all the way down to the backs of his knees, starting out green with a pink tip to match his ears. But it's not attached to the jockstrap.

It's coming from inside him.

My mouth is dry as I step closer, my eyes glued to him as he moves onto his knees, stretching his arms out on the bed. Then he sticks his ass up, and I know full well that he's completely aware of how much he's showing off his new gear. We haven't done anything penetrative yet, not even with fingers. Now I come in here and find he's got god knows how big a plug shoved up his ass that he's currently teasing me with.

Everything I ever said about going slow vanishes in an instant. My kitten is clearly setting the pace here, and it's now my job to give him every single thing he desires.

I run my hand over the smooth skin along his spine, loving the way he shivers at my touch. He turns and rises up on his knees, his hands landing on my chest where he starts to paw at my T-shirt, then he gently bats my face.

"Hey, baby," I say softly, drinking in every second and committing it to memory. This is easily one of the sexiest things I've ever seen with my own two eyes. Between my legs, my cock is throbbing, desperate to be released. There's a real danger that whatever happens next, I'm going to have to fight hard not to blow my load immediately.

Usually, Jessie's mouth is running a mile a minute and he has whole conversations all by himself. But tonight, he hasn't spoken a word yet. I wonder how deep he's already gotten himself into kitten headspace or if he's purposefully trying to push himself there now. I stroke his hair, watching all his quirky little cat movements.

"You're beautiful," I murmur without even realizing I've spoken. His eyes flick to meet mine, so I carry on. "Good kitty. Such a pretty kitty for Daddy."

He nuzzles his nose against my cheek, making that adorable little purring noise that he's become so adept at. His lips seek out mine, kissing me deeply as I run my hands up his sides, my thumbs finding the bars in his nipples to rub. He meows into my mouth, humping himself against my thigh.

Without warning, he drops down, pressing kisses against my stomach. My T-shirt is getting in the way, so I whip it off and allow his warm lips and hot breath access to my skin.

He takes advantage of that by biting my hip.

Not hard. But enough for me to get little indents from his teeth pressed into my flesh.

"Bad kitty," I say with an arched eyebrow, wondering how far he's going to push this. So far, he's not been much of a brat, but I've wondered if one is lurking under the surface.

He looks up at me for a second, biting down harder. Just when I'm about to tap his nose, he lets go and begins licking the spot with small flicks of his tongue. I moan and thread my fingers through his hair, careful not to disturb the headband his ears are attached to.

I love the gentle quietness between us as he kisses and sucks the hickey onto my skin. I've marked kittens before in different ways, but no one's ever done this for me. It makes me feel strange, but in a good way. He's claiming me. He wants me.

This was a boy who didn't even really understand what being a kitten meant a few weeks ago. Now I look down and watch him swishing his gorgeous tail as he turns in a circle, mimicking so many pretty cat movements with his hands and his head as he continues to purr. When he comes back around, he nuzzles his face against my stomach before latching his teeth onto the top of my jeans and starting to tug.

I think it's adorable that he wants to try and undress me without using his hands. I can see how that would help him feel more kitteny. But that button is going to be hard to pop, and selfishly, I'm too hard to enjoy watching him try.

"Here," I grunt, slipping my fingers between his face and my belly, deftly releasing the button at the top before cradling the side of his face against my palm. "Such a good kitty for Daddy."

He grins before licking and nipping at my hand. Then he's back to my zipper, dragging it down with his teeth, pulling my jeans down a little as well to give me more freedom. I gasp as he attacks my briefs next, and before I know it, my hard, leaking cock has sprung free.

He hums in delight as he rests his two gloved hands against my hips, then wraps his lips around my member, swallowing me down as far as possible. I hiss and grab his hair, not wanting to come right away. This is too good to ruin prematurely.

"Good boy," I say over and over. "Good boy for Daddy."

Just as I'm starting to get dangerously close, he pops off and gives me a devilish grin, saliva and pre-cum glistening on his chin. As I try to catch my breath, he bounds over to the nightstand, where I see he's left a single condom in its foil packet. Very carefully, he picks it up with his teeth, then comes trotting back over to me, holding it up proudly.

I take it from him and wipe his face clean. "Do you want Daddy to fuck you, little kitty?" I ask gently, my voice low. I can hear my own desperation, and there's no sense in fighting it. I want my baby boy so badly it hurts.

He rises up, placing his hands on my chest as he climbs up my body, planting a kiss on my jaw. He looks me in the eyes and nods before twisting around and flopping onto his stomach. The beautiful fluffy tail sticks up proudly from in between his cheeks. I think about how he worked that inside himself, just for me. How he waited up here for me to come home, just so he could surprise me.

I am going to give him the best night of his life.

In no time at all, I've got the rest of my clothes off and I'm climbing on top of him. Carefully, I place his hands above his head and ease his legs apart. Then I fetch some lotion from the drawer that has a beautiful macadamia nut-and-vanilla scent that's rich without being too sickly sweet. Squirting some onto my hands, I position myself behind him and start to massage the backs of his legs.

The moans that fill the air are utterly obscene. I have no trouble staying hard as my gorgeous kitten writhes and whimpers underneath me. He works and trains so hard it often leaves him tense, so one of my favorite things is to massage his tired muscles. By the time I'm done, he's a puddle of goo, just the way I want him.

"Good boy," I murmur as I knead his ass cheeks. "Such a good boy for your Daddy."

Making sure I have the lube and condom at hand, I begin to ease the plug from his hole, telling him to relax and reminding him just how beautiful he is. By the time I free the reasonably sized metal bulb, his whimpers are almost sobs, so I take a moment to stop and kiss his cute little bubble butt.

"Are you ready for Daddy, kitten?" I ask, placing the luxurious tail on the other nightstand out of our way. He turns his head to one side and nods lethargically. "Good boy."

My hands are trembling as I suit up and drizzle lubricant over both my dick and his puffy little pucker, which is already so nicely stretched out. It's been so long since I made love with anyone, and I'm desperate to make Jessie feel amazing. But I'm also ravenous for him, and I can barely contain myself as I start to sink into his hot, greedy hole.

"Fuck," I groan, dropping my head back and screwing up my eyes. Even with the rubber on, he feels amazing. Despite his blissed-out state, he's getting onto his knees and backing up against me so I can thrust farther inside him. I run my hands along his sides, loving how damp his skin is. Our heavy pants fill the air, our perspiration mixing in with the scent of the lotion, lube, and burning candle wicks.

"Daddy," he whispers, the first word he's spoken all evening. My heart flips in my chest and I lean down to wrap my arms around his chest and hug him from behind.

"I'm here, baby," I assure him. He lets out a long moan as I bottom out, my cock nestling inside him like he was made to hold me. "You're perfect," I manage to grunt. Honestly, the fact that I can even get a single syllable out right now is impressive.

"Daddy," he utters again, pushing against me, looking for movement.

I give it to him.

He's obviously been worked up for a while, and I've been on a hair trigger, even before his lips touched my cock. So I begin to thrust, gripping his hips tightly so I can piston as hard and fast as he can take. From the way he starts squealing and thrashing, I know I've found his prostate, and my heart overflows with joy knowing that he's losing his mind because of me.

I know I wanted to wait because I was afraid we were moving things too fast. He'd only been living with me a couple of weeks before we started dating, and we've never even had a conversation about how to label it because I was afraid that would put too much pressure on him.

But in this moment, I just know he's mine, all mine. I'll do anything for him. I'll treasure him and pleasure him and give him everything I've got. No way I'm messing this up like last time. If I have to push myself out of my comfort zone for him, I will. He deserves that. He deserves everything.

It might only be my inner monologue but I'm aware I'm babbling, even if it's just to myself. I'm losing my mind with desire as my orgasm builds, waves of ecstasy crashing over me until, finally, it explodes.

I can't remember the last time I came so hard. Certainly not from my own hand. It feels like it goes on for minutes as I shoot again and again into the condom buried in my little kitten's ass. It's probably only twenty to thirty seconds, but when I eventually come to a shuddering stop, my body draped over Jessie's, I have to take a few seconds to properly catch my breath. I feel like I've been hit with a wrecking ball.

And I'm not the only one. Underneath me, Jessie is a quivering mess, and as I trail my hands over his taut body, I discover quickly that he's still rock hard, waiting to come.

Good. I want to be the one to draw it out of him.

Carefully, I extract myself from him, quickly pull off the condom, tie it up, then throw it into the trash can in the en suite. While I'm there, I grab a washcloth to dampen, come back and gently clean up his behind. Then I ease him onto his back, hooking my fingers over the satin jockstrap, and drag it down over his hips and thighs before discarding it onto the floor.

His cock is straining and red, shiny with precum, and jerking in anticipation. But I can't help but give each of his nipples a good suck first, rolling my tongue over those tantalizing piercings. He might be shattered, but he still squirms underneath me, his loose limbs twitching as he gasps and moans.

I don't torture him for long, taking pity and swallowing his delicious cock down in one go. He cries out, his body jerking off the bed before dropping back down again. I hold his hip to keep him steady, bobbing my head and sucking as hard as I can. In no time at all, he's spurting down my throat, and I drink every last drop.

By the time I come up to kiss his lips, he's almost passed out already. I chuckle, close to falling asleep myself. But I take the time to undress him and wipe off any other mess before snuggling up behind him, hugging him close, and draping a blanket over both of us. It's still pretty early in the evening, but I figure if we wake up for a midnight snack, that's no big deal.

Right now, I just need to keep my precious kitten in my arms and never let him go.

It startles me how much I mean that literally.

CHAPTER 16

Jessie

I SPEND THE NEXT SEVERAL DAYS IN A DREAM, FLOATING around in my own happy little bubble. Nothing can touch me. When I arrived in Paddle Creek, I thought my life had crumbled around my ankles and that there would be no way to recover. Now I have a stable home, I'm thriving at school, I'm cheering again, and I've got the most incredible, wonderful, sexy Daddy a kitten could ever ask for.

Don't get me wrong. It's not all sunshine and rainbows. Half the time, cheer training is more stressful than it is productive. The team just doesn't have a lot of experience, and although plenty of them are quite talented dancers and gymnasts, there's just a lack of cohesion when it comes to stunting.

It's not hard to understand why. Lakelyn is a terrific performer in her own right and has a great attitude, but sadly she's a bit too nice and doesn't yell at people when they're being disrespectful. She's only been captain since the start of this semester, so she's still cutting her teeth in. I know she's going to be awesome once she finds her feet. But the squad itself isn't very disciplined.

Tara, on the other hand, doesn't have any trouble chewing people out, especially when they don't deserve it.

For a while, I just kept my head down and tried to fix things from within by coaching my own stunt group. But the funny thing about having a calm (albeit cat-filled) home and the devotion of a good man is that suddenly I've got about a hundred percent more energy than I've been operating with throughout the duration of my mom's illness. Not to mention a hundred percent less tolerance for bullshit since the crap Parker pulled with me.

I don't like bullies.

Today's training session isn't going well. It's supposed to be a game-day practice, but our competition routine is in such a shambles that Lakelyn is using the last half an hour to try and work on our pyramid. The Snowdown is only a month away now, and we're so not ready.

It just so happens that my base partner couldn't make it today, so Alannah is stepping in as a substitute. This is why we're friends. No matter how crushed she was not to make the comp squad, she's always the first to training and gives a thousand percent, no matter what.

The trouble is that you and your stunt group can be as brilliant as you like. If the flyer next to you in the formation is determined to drag your girl down every time she goes up, everyone's face-planting on the mat.

"Get it together, Connick!" Tara shrieks at Alannah. "You can't bitch about not making the team if you can't even put up a decent liberty extension!"

Lakelyn waves her hands. "Come on, everyone, that's not productive. Why don't we...um...?"

But seeing Alannah close to tears makes me snap. I know Lakelyn is just trying to keep the harmony for the whole squad, but Tara shouldn't be allowed to crush people's spirits just because she's somehow managed to weasel her way onto the committee.

"There are four people in our stunt group and our lib is solid," I say firmly, glaring at Tara. "Perhaps we should go over timings as a team to make sure the whole formation is secure?"

I don't want to throw our neighboring group under the bus. But I'm also not willing to take the blame for something that isn't our fault either.

"Oh," Tara says in a dangerously fake nice tone. "You're on the coaching team now, are you, Garras? Well, if you know everything, why don't you just come over here and—"

"Tara, enough!" Lakelyn cries in a rare display of frustration and annoyance. The entire room goes quiet. "I'm the captain, and I think drilling timings might actually help us."

"I think so, too!" Professor Ulman pipes up from the bleachers, raising her hand. "Remember my 'no ER' rule, people."

Tara gives Lakelyn a tight smile as she crosses her arms. "Fine," she snips, then shoots me a glare before marching off to join her gang of lemmings that all give me the stink eye as well.

It's nice to be popular.

Despite the tense atmosphere, we start marking the pyramid with our flyers standing on the ground in front of us as we practice the arm movements. It becomes obvious very quickly that some people are unsure or, worse, are confidently getting the motions wrong. But by the end of the session, we've got it pretty solid and even manage to do a shaky run-through of the sequence where no one falls to the ground.

I call that a win.

"Thanks, Jessie," Lakelyn says warmly to me as we're packing up our gear.

I shake my head. "You killed it, babe," I tell her.

She grins and walks off, an extra spring in her step.

I deliberately don't look around to see Tara's or her gang's reaction. Instead, I wait until Alannah is ready to head out, then loop my arm through hers. "You also killed it today, you know," I tell her.

She sighs and shrugs. "Maybe? Thank you. I just wish it was enough."

We've talked at length about how she doesn't want me to feel guilty for getting a spot when she didn't, so I simply hold space for her to be sad. It isn't fair. There are definitely people on the comp squad only because they're friends with Tara and the other popular girls. I really thought we'd left all that shit in high school.

When you've held the hand of someone fighting for their life, that kind of petty politics is so astronomically unimportant.

"Just keep being you and they have no choice but to promote you when a spot becomes available," I assure her. "Besides, Tara's leaving next year, so fuck her."

"No thanks," Alannah says as her standard retort, grinning.

I laugh as well as we push our way through the doors and into the twilight. Fall is coming in fast these days, but the weather hasn't quite turned yet.

"Hey," I say, a sudden thought occurring to me. "Nim gave me this voucher thingy for a local salon. I think he wants to encourage me to stop chewing my nails." I chuckle ruefully because he's right. But there's warmth in my heart because what he actually said was that beautiful kitties should have beautiful claws. It's crazy how treasured he's made me feel in such a short time. "Do you want to come with me?"

Alannah might be a rock chick, but she does tend to paint her nails. She raises her eyebrows at me, then looks down at her chipped polish. "Oh. Uh…yeah. That sounds lovely. But it's your present from your boyfriend. I can pay for myself."

I shake my head and sidestep the boyfriend comment. We still haven't officially labeled anything yet. I tell myself that's fine, but it might be nice to have the assurance that Nim sees this as something real enough to have words for it.

"We can use the voucher for both of us, then split whatever it doesn't cover," I insist. "Then maybe we can go for ice cream after."

"Or Creams!" she suggests enthusiastically.

I laugh along with her, glad she's on board. "Hell yeah."

It's almost a shame that I have a car and a reserved parking spot right in the middle of town. Paddle Creek has a rickety old tram system like something out of Europe. I've never seen anything like it in real life. Sure, it looks like I'd be putting my life on the line just by riding it. But it also looks kind of fun.

Today, though, I take myself and Alannah from the gym into town where we can walk from the back of Toe Beans to a place called Butterflies. Like everything around here, it looks like it might have once been pretty slick. Perhaps back in the eighties. Unfortunately, the 'f' on the pink sign has broken so it now reads 'Butter-lies' which is kind of funny.

What's more evident as we approach, though, is that there's a young guy washing the front windows, and it's not just regular maintenance. They've been egged.

Alannah and I stop outside, both staring sadly at the damage some little shits have done. There are wet piles of toilet paper on the sidewalk that I assume the guy has already pulled down. But worse than that is the word he's halfway through scrubbing off. All I can see is -ore. I assume that the missing letters are a 'w' and an 'h.'

"Oh, man," Alannah says, getting the guy's attention. "Do you need a hand?"

His head snaps around from where he's perched on the ladder. I'd guess he was in his late teens and probably doesn't really know how cute he is yet. He's still got that gangly ugly duckling air about him. But with his square jaw and sparkling eyes, he'll probably be breaking hearts in no time.

"Hey, there!" he says brightly. "That's kind of you, but I'm okay. You here to see my mom?"

I frown. "Uhh…?"

He laughs. "She runs the salon. Are you here for some pampering?"

"Oh!" I say with a grin. "Yeah, for sure."

The guy indicates the front door with the hand still holding his sponge, flicking water through the air. The bucket of water is perched precariously on top of the steps, and I pray it won't topple down onto his sneakers.

"Head right on in," he says cheerfully. "We haven't had many customers today on account of…well…" He looks glumly back at the window.

"People are such dicks," I tell him. "I'm so sorry."

He shrugs and smiles, clearly trying not to let the bastards get him down. "I'll have it right again in no time. I just hope they don't come back tonight."

He sighs before dunking his sponge into the bucket and continuing with his scrubbing.

"Good luck," Alannah says as we head for the door.

"Catch you later," I add, and we share a nod.

Inside Butterflies is a riot. Zebra print walls, mirror balls hanging from the ceiling, and about a hundred plastic orchids in various colors greet us. An eighties power ballad is playing softly over the sound system. The only lighting comes from lamps with stands in the shape of sparkly pink legs wearing black stilettos, fringe hanging from the bottom of the black lamps.

A woman in her forties jumps up from behind the desk.

Half her poodle perm is tied in a scrunchie, and her dark eyeliner is about half an inch thick all around. She wears sparkly pink pumps that fit in well with the décor, along with black leather pants and a faded Blondie T-shirt. Tattoos cover her arms, mostly of sunken ships and mermaids.

"Hi, there!" she cries. "You looking to get your nails fixed?"

I glance around at the empty shop. There aren't any other customers, and she's the only employee out here.

I glance at Alannah, thinking of the voucher I've got on my phone. Alannah gives me two thumbs-up. "Fingers *and* toes," I say cheerfully.

The woman clutches her hands to her chest. "God bless you. Let's get you settled. In fact, since it's just us gals, let's have a VIP day, hmm? You kids old enough for some bubbles?"

Like half the people at the college, Alannah worked for a couple of years beforehand, so we both nod eagerly. Soon enough, we're set up in chairs with our feet in warm, bubbling water, each with a glass of cheap but tasty Champagne in our hands as the lady starts working on Alannah's nails, and I wait my turn. She's got an LED lamp so she can see what she's doing while keeping the atmosphere of the rest of the salon.

"So I'm Candy," the woman says, "and this here's been my pride and joy for over fifteen years. You kids at the college, I take it?"

"Yes, ma'am," I say politely. "We're both liberal arts majors on the cheerleading squad."

Candy gasps and looks at me with glossy eyes. "No kidding? *I* was a Kitten back in the day! Oh my god, we're sisters!"

Alannah and I both laugh, but actually the sentiment is warm and heartfelt.

"Cheers to that," I say, clinking my glass against Alannah's and then Candy's coffee mug.

"Well, if any of your pals need a bit of glam, you tell them to come here for a discount, okay?" Candy says as she buffs and primes Alannah for her first coat.

Because of cheer, neither of us can have our nails long, but Candy has promised us gorgeous gels nonetheless. Alannah is going for an extremely cool sort of French manicure where her nails are mostly black with red tips. I think I might get little paw prints on mine because I'm nothing if not predictable.

"We definitely will," I tell Candy, thinking of the many really nice members of the Kittens and ignore all thoughts of Tara and her minions. They would undoubtedly turn their noses up at a place like Butterflies. In fact, part of me wants to check their alibis for the time of the vandalism outside.

"I'm sorry about the damage," I say sincerely. "The guy outside seems confident he can fix it, though."

"Oh, you met Shawn," she says excitedly. "That's my boy, my angel. His daddy was a good-for-nothing cheating snake, but Shawn is the best thing that ever happened to me. I told him he can go anywhere he wants next year, but he keeps saying he's gonna go to school here so he can stick around and help his momma. Such a good boy."

Her tone is wistful, and my heart aches as I think about my own mom. We've talked a ton on the phone over the past few weeks. She knows school is going well and was thrilled I made the team.

But she doesn't know about Nim.

It's not that I'm ashamed or embarrassed by what we have. Nothing like that. I'm just not sure if there's anything to tell. I know we spend a lot of time together, and the intimacy we share is unbelievable.

I'm just not sure if I can tell my mother I have a boyfriend or not.

Those thoughts aren't helpful right now, so I shake them away. "He's lucky to have you," I say earnestly to Candy.

"Aw, shucks," she says with a wave of her hand. "We're a team. We do okay. It's just lately…well, all this business with the mayor is damn hard on *my* business. On everyone's."

I frown and glance at Alannah. But she shakes her head, so we both look back at Candy. "The mayor?" I ask. This is the first I've even heard mention of them.

She huffs and scowls, working on painting Alannah's nails as she talks. "Oh, Mayor Durham has got some bee in his bonnet about us Cardinals. Thinks all bikers are suddenly criminals. We can't prove nothing, of course. But ever since he started his reelection campaign, we've all been getting complaints and protests and shit like you saw outside. He's just tryna drag us all down."

My heart rate has picked up. She's talking about Nim's chapter. His family. "Us?" I ask.

She nods. "A bunch of the gang own businesses here in town, not just me. There's the pub, O'Toole's, Horowitz's garage, the Toe Beans café—"

"Toe Beans?" I squeak.

She nods. "The mayor's damn wife is on a health and safety rampage, tryna prove the place is unsanitary. Horse hooey. Me and my girls go there every single Thursday for red velvet cupcakes before rockaoke at O'Toole's." She wags a finger at me. "If the Durhams try and mess with rockaoke cupcake day, there's going to be serious consequences."

I try and laugh along with her, but I can feel Alannah looking at me in concern. Nim hasn't mentioned any of this. I don't want to think he's been lying to me after everything Parker put me through, but…

"I just think the mayor is tryna run us all out of business,"

Candy continues. "That way, his buddy McKenna can buy up all the property and do nothing with it, as usual."

"McKenna?" Alannah says. "I know that name."

"Rafferty McKenna," Candy explains. "He thinks Paddle Creek is his own personal Monopoly board. Doesn't give a shit about the people. He's just waiting until he's got enough property so he can raze the whole place to the ground and start over with fancy gated communities and shit. Says the land is good but the eighties ruined all the real estate." She snorts. "As if."

"What?" I say in horror. "Why would he do that? Why would *anyone* do that?"

Candy shrugs. "When you live up in your ivory tower, you lose compassion. Empathy. He probably thinks we'll all thank him for it, like he's the king of the castle, and we're all just his peasants." She gives me a sly look. "I studied history, though. The thing about peasants is that if you treat 'em badly enough, they eventually revolt."

"Guillotine time," Alannah says with a cackle.

I laugh along with them, but I'm quickly lost in thought as the conversation moves onto music. They chat about an all-girl pop-rock band called Glittergasm that I vaguely remember touring with Below Zero when I saw them back in the day. Normally, I'd love to gush over my favorite ladies in music, but I'm too preoccupied worrying about concerns closer to home.

Is Nim's beloved café really in trouble because of some political bullshit? And, more importantly, if it *is...*

Why hasn't he told me about it?

CHAPTER 17

Nim

I WILL NEVER, EVER COMPLAIN ABOUT THE INCREDIBLE SEX Jessie and I are having, nor the wonderful frequency of it.

But trying to change the bed sheets with ten cats around is just a little bit challenging, I must admit. Even with several spare sets to rotate, the fact that I'm now doing it at least two or three times a week doesn't seem to be dampening any of my furry friends' enthusiasm for it. Or mine for having sex.

Hell, right now, we're on our third day in a row of fresh bedding.

"Libra, really?" I say in exasperation. I've managed to get the fresh sheet on, and the pillowcases didn't need changing. But trying to wrestle the duvet cover on is proving to be some kind of military operation. Currently, I've got two cats inside the damn thing, with a third on top, batting at them through the cover.

"Hello?"

All my stress melts away in a flash at hearing Jessie's voice. "In here!" I call out, giving up and dropping the whole duvet to the floor. Jessie knows by now not to step on the bedding when it's deconstructed because it will inevitably be filled with felines. I turn just as he comes through the door.

Immediately, I reach for his hands, looking at the beautiful job Candy's done with my kitten's nails. It distressed me how he would anxiously chew on them, so we agreed that this might be a nice way to help him break the habit. Plus, I get the satisfaction of knowing that I've marked him. This adorable manicure signals to the world that he's mine.

They're teal and purple, just like his squad colors, and each nail has the top half of a tiny cat face poking up from different positions around the edge of his nail. I think they're adorable. I look up, expecting him to be giddy and excited.

But his eyes are wide and…wet?

Oh god!

"Baby, what's wrong?" I cry, grabbing his shoulders.

He looks away from me and chews his lip. My heart is breaking just looking at him, but anger is also rising. If someone's hurt him, I will kick down their door to give them a piece of my mind if I have to.

"Why didn't you tell me about Mayor Durham?" he asks quietly.

I blink, his words not making any sense. "Huh?" I grunt.

He huffs and turns back to frown at me. "You didn't tell me that he's been terrorizing the Cardinals for weeks! That his wife is trying to get Toe Beans shut down! You *lied* to me!"

I feel like I've been slapped in the face. "No, no!" I splutter. "I…"

But he's right.

I might not have exactly been lying to him. But I haven't told him the whole truth, either.

Hanging my head in shame, I rub my thumbs against his shoulders. "Oh, kitten. I'm so sorry. I was just trying to protect you."

"From what?" he demands. "Real life? This isn't just some kinky thing to me, Nim. I'm *with* you. I want to be a part of your life. But if that's not what you want, if you want to shut me out—"

"NO!" I shout, my heart threatening to explode out of my chest. I take a deep breath as Jessie looks at me, startled. "I shouldn't have shouted. I'm sorry. No, baby, I want you in every part of my life. This is real for me. I'm all in. But *I'm* supposed to protect you, to provide for *you*. I didn't know if my whole life was about to implode, and I didn't want to burden you with that."

Mercifully, Jessie finally sighs and looks at me with affection. "I'm not with you for any of those reasons, Nim," he says, sounding slightly exasperated. "Yes, I love it that you take care of me. You're the kindest, sweetest, most selfless man I've ever met. But I'm with you because you're *you*. I don't want you shielding me like I'm some fragile child—"

"I don't think that," I interrupt hotly.

Jessie raises an eyebrow. "Well, that's exactly how I feel right now. Candy seems like a lovely lady, but she's not who I want to hear my Daddy's most important news from."

My shoulders slump. "Oh," I say. He has a good point. "Okay. Fair enough."

"Nim?" he says, sounding so unsure and small it brings a lump to my throat.

"Yes, baby?" I reply. I lift my right hand from his shoulder to cup the side of his face.

He hesitates for a moment, looking away. "What can I call you?"

For a moment, I'm confused. "Daddy," I say eventually, feeling like I'm missing something.

Sure enough, he's still looking away, but now he bites his lip. "I mean to other people. Are you...are you my boyfriend? Are we exclusive?"

If I felt like an idiot before, it's absolutely nothing to the mortification that rushes through me right then. I pull him against me in a crushing hug, burying my face against his neck as he clings to me.

"Oh, baby boy," I cry in anguish. "You're my everything! That's what being your Daddy means to me. You can call me your boyfriend or your partner or whatever. I am totally devoted to you, and the fact that you didn't already know that breaks my heart."

He lets out a sob against my chest, and I just hold him even tighter. I'm so ashamed of myself. This is why Brent left. I'm terrible at getting what's out of my head into the world. I thought Jessie understood what we were, but obviously, I wasn't clear enough.

I'm a bad Daddy.

"I'm so sorry," I utter again, my throat thick. "I let you down."

He shakes his head. "I was too afraid to ask," he says with a hiccup. "It's my fault. I'm sorry I called you a liar."

"I will *never* lie to you," I promise him, kissing down his jaw until he turns his head slightly and allows me to capture his mouth. I claim him with a terrified sort of passion. I could have *lost* him because I'm such an ass. "You have nothing to apologize for," I reassure him.

"I was afraid to ask for what I wanted," he says, his glassy eyes searching mine. "I thought if we didn't label it, then it couldn't be a rejection. I thought I was okay with that. I didn't want to rush it."

"Me neither," I admit.

He chuckles and rolls his eyes. "Yeah, and then we both jumped in feet first anyway." I laugh with him, not denying it. However, then he exhales and looks more seriously at me. "Nim, you know that Parker hurt me. But that was more because he left me out on the streets. I...I don't think I ever felt about him the way I do about you. I hope that's okay to say."

I sigh and rub my thumb against his cheekbone. "That's definitely okay," I say. "I…um, I care about you a lot, Jessie."

I'm worried that I shouldn't be saying things like that so soon. I don't want to pressure him or scare him off. From the look on his face, however, I suspect it was exactly the right thing to say. I'm fretting about overwhelming him when actually what he probably needs is *more* assurance after what his ex pulled on him.

"I'm the luckiest kitten in the world," Jessie says with a sweet smile as he rubs my back.

I shake my head. "Nuh-uh. I'm the luckiest Daddy," I insist, leaning down to capture his lips again.

It isn't long before our kisses become frantic, and soon we're pulling off each other's clothes in a mad rush. As we tumble onto the bed, I get the feeling neither of us wants to mess around too much with preparation. So I just pin him to the bed, smothering him, showing him who he belongs to as I wrap my hand around both our cocks.

We thrust together and pant into each other's mouths. I steady myself above him with my free hand, and he digs his fingers into my back, scratching me with his new manicure.

I love it. I want his claw marks on me all the time.

Sometimes our lovemaking is slow and luxurious. This is desperate and raw. As he starts to come, I kiss his neck and hold him close, telling him how good and perfect he is. And that he's mine.

Mine, mine, *mine.*

Once he's spent, he flops back down on the mattress with a full-body shudder, his chest covered in his mess. He's so beautiful it takes my breath away. How he could have even thought for one second that I wasn't in this a hundred percent with him breaks my heart.

I'll have to do better from now on.

I take myself in hand and stare down at him as I chase my own climax. It doesn't take long before I'm painting him with long white ropes that splatter across his skin and the surrounding sheet like he's my own personal work of art. He never takes his eyes off me, looking up at me through dark eyelashes.

My heart stutters as the last of my seed spills. I know I'm looking down at him lovingly as well.

Because I love him.

The realization terrifies me because in the next breath I know how it would destroy me to lose him. I've never felt so wholly enveloped by someone else in my entire life. The emotion is too much. Rather than pay too close attention to it, I lean down and press my lips against his, kissing him tenderly.

"Sweetheart," I say breathlessly.

"Daddy," he mumbles back, pulling me down to hug him despite all the mess we've made. I wrap him in my arms and roll us onto our sides to cradle him against me. Cum drips down and makes the sheet even wetter, but I don't care.

My boy needs me.

"I'm here, kitten," I assure him as he starts to shake. He's crying again, but this time, I hope it's from the relief of letting go of all of those pent-up emotions he'd been carrying around. "Daddy's here. You're okay."

I decide to bring him into a nice hot shower. Not only will it clean us up, but I think he'll find it soothing. He's clearly been through a bit of an emotional roller coaster today, and I suspect he's going to need a little time to process all of it.

I know I've fucked up. Words like 'boyfriend' don't resonate with me, so I've rarely used them outside of my teen years. 'Daddy' means so much more. But obviously, Jessie was feeling insecure about our commitment to each other despite it being totally clear to me what was going on.

"My kitten," I tell him again as I'm drying him off. I hope he'll understand soon what I mean when I say that. That's a promise of my devotion. I'm his Daddy, and I want to take care of everything I can for him. I want to be his all, his one and only.

"Daddy," he says with deep sincerity as he looks into my eyes. I'll never get tired of hearing that word from his pretty lips.

I'm devastated I let him down. He's right. I should have been open and talked to him about the war Mayor Durham is waging against me and my friends—my family. I tried to shelter him because I wanted to protect him, but in doing so, I shut him out of really significant events happening in my life right now.

There might be a certain power dynamic at play in our relationship, but he's got a point. I should treat him like an equal, not like a delicate thing I need to censor hard truths from.

It goes to show how afraid I truly am. Not just of what Durham could do to me, my business, and my friends' busi-nesses. But of how I feel about Jessie. Contrary to what the fuck-ups I can now see clearly might indicate, I don't want to blow this. I'll do everything in my power to be good enough for Jessie and keep him by my side.

So we can have a talk now about all the things I've been hiding from him, and he can ask me any questions he needs to. I'll do my best to answer him fully.

But first, we have to change the bed sheet.
Again.

CHAPTER 18

Jessie

"Thanks so much again for helping me out," I tell Leah as we make our way into the college cafeteria. "I'm sure these will be a treat!"

Toe Beans might get its baked goods delivered to the café, but Nim's colleague spent all morning with me making trays of rainbow-frosted cupcakes for the Kittens' bake sale this afternoon. I might love eating cake, but honestly, I have no idea how to make it, and definitely not well. But Leah jumped at the chance to help me.

"I'm glad to do it," she insists as we carefully place the boxes down on the table where the other volunteers will arrange them to sell. "I love working at the café, don't get me wrong. But baking is my happy place. And helping your team out is good karma."

She tucks a blonde curl behind her ear and looks around the cafeteria. Lakelyn and the committee have done a great job setting up signs and balloons to decorate the usually pretty gray room. We're doing our best to raise some cash to help with our transportation to the Snowdown in a few weeks. Our usual bus company accidentally double-booked us, apparently, so we're having to fork out extra in order to get a last-minute replacement.

I think about Leah this morning, covered in flour in her kitchen, squealing in delight when the rainbow frosting came out of the piping bag just right. She definitely was in her happy place.

It makes me reflect on my own new happy place. In my former life, I would have said it was on the competition mat with my old school team, especially that moment when you finish a routine and know you've hit it perfectly, only to turn around and see everyone celebrating and realize they did, too.

In recent years, it been a bit different. A bit quieter. My happy place was sitting out on the back porch with Mom, watching the sunset as we sipped on iced tea. But her illness always loomed, and it wasn't until this past summer that we could do that and truly be content, knowing that she'd beaten that son of a bitch.

Now? God. That's an easy one. My happy place is when I'm in full kitten mode with my Daddy doting on me. It's the purest bliss I could ever imagine.

I'm so glad we talked after my mani-pedi last week. He really seemed to understand why I was so upset with him. I almost felt bad, though, when I realized he definitely didn't know that *I* didn't know how much of a thing we were. Apparently, asking to be my Daddy was a Big Deal, and from that point in his mind we were 'going steady,' as my mom would say.

But now I know. I've been practicing calling him my boyfriend by dropping it into conversation with people over the past few days. The first time I tried it with Alannah, she squealed and practically knocked me over with her hug, so I'd say that was a success. I even mentioned to my mom that I might be seeing someone. I'm still too apprehensive to give her the full details, but it's a start at least.

I regret calling him a liar. He's nothing like Parker. And it wasn't like he was telling me things that weren't true. He was just avoiding mentioning events that were upsetting him and out of his control. Now I think he gets why that was bad. If we're a real couple, then I want to help shoulder his burdens, not be an additional one for him.

The trouble is he was partly right. There isn't anything I can do to help the situation either, and now I'm just worrying about it as well. It's so incredibly unfair that the mayor has decided to use the Cardinals as a scapegoat to try and get himself reelected when he could be focusing on a real problem like all the dilapidated services and buildings in the town.

It makes sense, though, if that McKenna guy is trying to bully enough places out of business so he can buy them up. It sounds like he's playing a long game to make serious money. In a way, it reminds me of that Richard Gere film where he buys up the companies to break them apart.

Maybe McKenna needs to meet a Julia Roberts to make him see the error of his ways and find a little humanity.

I'm drawn from my thoughts as Leah and I are walking past the library, and suddenly Clayton the raccoon pops out again in front of us. Leah and I both gasp and jump, but he doesn't pay any attention to us. He's too busy dashing around the side of the library with what looks like some sort of dishcloth in his mouth. It's trailing under his body between his legs as he runs out of sight.

"Weird," Leah says with a chuckle, shaking her head. "I've only ever seen him carrying food."

"Yeah, I saw him with a whole box of chicken tenders last week," I admit. "Before that, it was cupcakes."

"All near here?" she asks with a raised eyebrow.

"Uh, yeah, actually," I admit. "I guess he lives close by?"

She shakes her head. "No, he lives by the dumpsters behind the east dorms. At least he did in my day. We used to feed him veggies and nuts and stuff." She rolls her eyes. "Of course some of the boys fed him popcorn and beef jerky, but I checked and technically it's not the worst for raccoons."

"So what's he doing hanging around here then?" I ask.

She nods thoughtfully. Without saying anything, we both begin to walk around the side of the library.

I didn't realize, but there's a secluded little rose garden. There's a pretty semicircle stone bench with carved legs to sit on and wind chimes hanging from brackets on the brick wall.

Among the flowers I see bright white stones nestled in winding patterns as well as little stone statues of what I think are trolls and goblins. Something about their chubby cheeks and naughty grins makes me think they're Scandinavian for some reason. Perhaps I saw them in a fairy tale book when I was little.

Some of the stones section off a rectangular herb garden. I don't know much, but I think I recognize lavender, mint, and chamomile. Next to that is a reasonably thick tree stump with a small door carved into it and creamy mushrooms that look like pancakes growing off the sides of the bark.

"Wow," Leah says.

"Right?" I agree. "Did you know this was here?"

She gives me a nervous laugh. "I've probably walked past here hundreds of times. Before today, I would have sworn it just led to a dingy alleyway. I never bothered taking a closer look."

"Huh," I say. "Weird."

"Speaking of which," Leah says as she looks around. "Where's our little thief gone?"

I frown and turn on the spot, scanning the foliage. "Oh my god. Look."

Underneath a shrub, behind a bed of purple pansies so dark they look almost black, is a nest. I have to crouch down to see properly, but the edge of the dishcloth is poking out of the foliage. All of a sudden, Clayton's bandit face pops out, and he hisses at us.

"Yikes," I say, jerking backward. Clayton comes farther out, wringing his little hands. As he does, he moves the branches around.

That's when I see a *lot* of empty food cartons, a bunch of old rags and clothes, and in the middle of it all lies a black cat.

I'm no expert, but from her distended belly and panting, I'd say she's in labor.

"Oh, fuck," I cry, looking up at Leah. "Uh…I think we might need help."

"Help with what?"

We both look behind us to see that small a Black woman with very short blonde hair has appeared. Her jeans are ripped in that artfully-on-purpose sort of way, and she's got several ear and facial piercings.

"Oh, hi," Leah says a little breathlessly. "Uh…do you know anything about cats?"

"Cats?" the young woman repeats. But she crouches down beside us to look under the bush and gasps. "Oh, right. I see what you mean."

Clayton is pacing anxiously behind us on all fours. I glance between him and the black mama cat, feeling a bit confused.

"He's not the…"

"Father?" Leah asks before both the women bust out laughing. "No, Jessie. That's not how nature works. But maybe he's been looking after her or something. He's certainly made her a nice place to give birth."

Yeah, she's got a point. I'm too anxious to be thinking straight. Of course raccoons and cats can't have babies. But maybe she's onto something in thinking for whatever reason our friendly little campus trash panda might be acting as a sort of stepdad.

Wild.

I bite my lip and worry we're not doing something we should be. I guess cats give birth alone all the time. They like to take themselves off to a secluded nook and just get on with it. But nature doesn't always get it right. Maybe we should fetch water or clean towels. Or maybe we should just keep our distance and let her get the hell on with it.

"I think the first one might be on the way?" Leah says, then glances over to our new friend. "So…were you headed to the library?"

"Uh," the woman says, looking a little bashful. "I was going to see if the librarian was there, actually. Sometimes I say hi."

"Oh, you know Ms. Maude?" I say with a smile. Thinking about it, of course this is her garden. It's got big witchy vibes.

"Ms. Maude?" Leah says, tilting her head in curiosity.

"The librarian," I elaborate before nodding at the stranger. "I'm Jessie, and this is Leah."

"Selena," the other woman says before her eyes go wide. "Oh, wow. I think that's a kitten."

We all peer under the bush, trying to get a good look. Clayton hops and chitters behind us like a dad pacing the corridor of a hospital. Sure enough, eventually, we get a glimpse of a mouse-sized thing. It looks like it's wrapped in a condom until Mama gnaws on the sack, and then suddenly it breaks, and there's a black kitten.

"Wow," I say, shaking my head. "I've never seen that before."

"Me, neither," Leah agrees. "The cats are all neutered and spayed by the time they get to the café."

Selena looks at her, then lifts her eyebrows. "Oh…you work at Toe Beans, do you?"

"We both do," I mumble, my attention back on the cat. We wait patiently as she continues to push, and after a while, we go through the whole thing again, this time ending up with what looks like it could be a tabby baby.

"I guess Papa was a ginger, huh?" I say to the mama as she studiously cleans her babies.

Clayton hops around us, checking out his friend's progress. From Mama's body language I get the feeling that she's done. Two seems a small number for a cat litter, but it's probably not that unusual.

"What do we do now?" Leah asks. "I don't want to just leave them here."

Selena and I both shake our heads. "Nim will probably know," I say. "We could call the café."

"I guess he'll tell us to take them to the shelter we work with," Leah says thoughtfully. "They'll probably want to check her and her babies over."

"I think that raccoon might have something to say if we try and relocate his little valentine," Selena says with a nervous chuckle.

"Hmm," I agree. "Not to mention what Mama might do if we stick our hands in there. I feel like we definitely need an expert who won't upset them."

Leah nods. "How about—"

"Ah, *there* you are," a female voice says behind me as fingers slide through my hair. Nails graze my scalp, and my breath hitches. "The lost black kitten. I knew the tea leaves never lie to me."

I blink as both Leah and Selena look above me with their mouths hanging open. I twist enough so I can see the newcomer, relief whooshing through me as I realize it's Ms. Maude, the librarian.

"Oh, hi!" I say. "Uh, did you say you were looking for a black cat? She's under here."

Ms. Maude gives my head a little scratch that sends shivers down my spine, then withdraws her hand from my hair. As usual, she's wearing a long black floaty skirt and heeled boots. Today, she's got a knitted sweater on top and a leather choker around her neck, all black, of course. Thinking about it, I know I've seen her several times, but I'm not sure if she's ever really noticed me until right now.

She crouches down beside me, tilting her head with a smile. "Good cat," she says warmly. "I thought you were ready. Were you waiting for your audience?"

The cat yawns widely and swishes her tail. "Oh, is she yours?" I ask, remembering the black cat that's always by her side.

However, Ms. Maude shakes her head. "No. I have already been chosen. But I've seen our guest around lately. She knew what she was doing."

Mama blinks slowly at the librarian before turning back to tend to her newborns.

"Oh, that's good," I say, even though I don't exactly feel reassured. Talking to Ms. Maude makes me feel like I'm missing half of what she's actually saying. "Do you know what we should do with her? We were thinking of taking her to the shelter, but—"

"No," Ms. Maude interrupts quietly but firmly. She's not looking at any of us. Her eyes are locked with the cat's green ones. "She has chosen you."

"Me?" I say.

She chuckles. "All three of you. Can't you see? You cannot abandon her now. It would upset the balance."

"Karma," Leah agrees in a knowing voice.

"Right…" Selena says. "Em, I know you know about these things, but…"

"Hush, child," she says warmly with a little smile. "I do know. You and she," she glances at Leah, "were brought here for the young. The black kitten will take the mother."

What she says sounds ridiculous until I realize she's looking at me. Am I the black kitten? I guess that makes sense as a nickname. I am a kitten with dark hair. She probably has no idea about my personal life, but I'm always wearing my cat ear headphones.

"I will?" I say faintly, thinking of the *ten* cats Nim already has.

Ms. Maude stands. "I shall fetch a basket. For now, the family will remain with me until the time is right." She smiles to herself and presses her hands together. "Yes. The tea leaves never lie. All I needed was a little patience."

She swishes off, and I watch her with a slightly slack jaw.

"What just happened?" Selena asks.

"Your girlfriend just dumped us all with a cat each," Leah says incredulously, but there's a hint of excitement in her eyes.

Selena sighs. "She's not my girlfriend. Believe me, I've tried."

"Well…I think we're all linked to her now in some way," I say. "At least if we want to adopt the cats like she suggested."

Leah bites her lip. "My new place *does* allow pets," she admits.

"And they are adorable," Selena adds.

The two women look at each other, and it could be my imagination, but I feel something stir between them. Then I look down at the cats and find Mama staring right back at me.

My breath hitches. I think about the ten black cats that Nim has back at his apartment, all named after the star signs. He skipped Cancer for obvious reasons. I was glad when I realized that. But then that just leaves…

"Pisces," I murmur.

Mama cat blinks at me.

I'm not sure I believe in fate or destiny or whatever. But somehow, Nim was there for me just when I needed him. Are the three of us perhaps in the right place and the right time for these little creatures as well? It's better for everyone if they get adopted directly, I have no doubt. If they go to the shelter, the chances are they might just come to Toe Beans anyway. If no one ever takes the black ones, Mama might just end up with Nim regardless.

Maybe the universe brought us into this little garden to save everyone that heartache. What if it's asking me to pay Nim's kindness forward? That sounds like the karma Leah is always talking about.

I don't have to decide right now. Things are so uncertain with all this nasty business from the mayor anyway. But as Ms. Maude comes back with a wicker basket and gently transfers mother and babies to it, I can't take my eyes off Mama. When Ms. Maude shoos us away so she can tend to the young, I find myself making a promise.

"See you soon, Pisces," I say.

CHAPTER 19

Nim

"COME ON, LITTLE FELLOW," I SAY, TRYING TO COAX THE TABBY kitten off the top of the fridge. I have no idea how he got back there, but it's dusty and he could fall down the back, so he really needs to get out. The trouble is he's scared now and keeps backing away from my hand as I attempt to reach him.

Luckily, it's before seven, so the café hasn't even opened yet. My staff is tending to the cats and setting up the counter to serve customers, but it's just Leah and me back here on the rescue mission.

"How did he even get back here?" Leah asks.

I grunt from my position up the ladder. It makes me nervous with all this health inspector nonsense. I've never had a cat make it through the anti-chamber into the food prep area. We need to get this little guy out of here as soon as possible. I'm trying to keep my stress levels in control, though, as I'll only frighten him more if I'm not careful.

"So," I say, picking up our previous conversation in an attempt to calm us all down. "You're getting your own kitten?"

"I don't know, maybe?" Leah says as I wiggle my fingers at the tabby.

"Because that witch told you that you were gonna keep it?"

She laughs nervously. "Nim, you don't understand. She's insanely hot. It's like she puts a spell on me whenever I see her. And it's not just me! There's this girl Selena who was there too, and she's, like, besotted with her as well." She sighs. "She and I are meeting up for coffee in a couple of days to discuss it all."

I look down over my shoulder and arch an eyebrow. "That sounds like a date."

"I don't know, maybe!" Leah says, throwing up her hands. I laugh and go back to my kitten conundrum. "Anyway. Whatever. Enough about my love life. How's yours?"

I'm glad she can't see my face or the grin that creeps onto it. "Better than ever," I confess.

"Aww," she coos genuinely. "Are you in *lurve?*"

I bite my lip and just look at the tabby for a second. "Umm…"

"Oh my god, you *are!*" She gasps. "Nim, this is amazing! I'm so happy for you."

I give up on my troublemaker for a second, reasoning that he might chill out enough to be scooped up if I do. "It's still early days," I say, warning myself as much as her not to get too excited.

"Have you told him you love him?" she asks, putting her hands on her hips.

I decide that maybe turning my attention back to the kitten is a good idea after all. "I don't want to pressure him."

Leah makes an exasperated sound. She probably makes an exasperated gesture as well, but I can't see it now that I'm squinting over the top of the mucky fridge again. The tabby crouches and swishes his tail. I don't care if he bites me. I'll pull him out by his teeth if I have to.

"Benjamin!" Leah cries. "Life is too short! If you love him, tell him! You never know what could happen next!"

Truer words were never spoken.

A pounding on the door resonates through the café so much we even hear it out here. I look down at Leah in alarm.

"I'll go check it out," Leah says hastily.

It's more difficult not to panic now. "Come on, little one," I say in a low rumble. "We have to go. You can do it."

The tabby lets out a teeny but ferocious meow. I respect his spirit. But there's unknown fuckery afoot, and I'd really rather get him back in my pocket.

"You can't go back there!" I hear Leah shout. "Stop!"

The kitchen doors fly open, letting in a couple of panicked cats. "NO!" I bellow. But the person standing before me with her hands clasped doesn't seem to care.

Mrs. Durham.

"I'm afraid I'm going to have to ask you to stop what you're doing immediately, Mr. Decker," she says in that insufferably prim tone of hers.

"Bite me," I growl as Leah also comes flying through the doors. "Grab the cats," I bark at her, my heart in my mouth.

Are the other cats okay?

If this awful woman has come crashing into the café, have any bolted out the front door?

I feel sick just considering it.

"I'm on it, boss!" Leah cries while Mrs. Durham splutters.

"I beg your pardon?" she shrieks at me. "You can't speak to me like that."

"I just did," I grunt, not even turning around to address her. "You're scaring my fucking cats."

The poor tabby is running back and forth, making it impossible for me to grab him. I don't want to hurt him with my big sausage fingers, so I'm doing my absolute best to be gentle. He's going to be traumatized by this. If it harms his chances of getting homed, I'll never let this woman forget it.

"Mr. Decker," she snaps. "I am here with the county office of environmental health. Your business has been deemed unfit for human use and must be shut down with immediate effect."

"What?" I yell at her.

It's the last straw for the poor tabby. He backs up too far...and then he's gone.

"NO!" I jump down from the ladder and rush to the side of the fridge. Luckily, I have access there and can see the little guy has broken his fall by grabbing hold of the radiator grate. That can get hot, though, so I shove my arm in and lift him up so he's finally safe in my arms.

He's shaking and trying to flee again, but I bundle him in my shirt pocket and cradle him next to my heart.

Mrs. Durham looks shocked, but when our gazes meet, her expression changes to frosty again. "That's exactly what I've been telling everyone. You claim that this area is sanitary, yet I come in here and find a feline already contaminating everything. Did you hear what I said about your imminent closure, Mr. Decker?"

"I don't give a shit," I snarl. Looking around, I'm relieved to see that Leah has managed to get our two frightened escapees into carriers, although not without several bloody scratches on her arms. "Did any get outside?" I ask, sick with worry.

She shakes her head. "I don't think so, but I reckon we should do a head count immediately."

"Agreed."

We both storm out of the kitchen, leaving a spluttering Mrs. Durham behind. She can do whatever the hell she likes.

All I care about is that every soul is present and accounted for.

The café is in chaos. My employees are running around after terrified cats. Several men in dowdy suits are taping up the front door as well as the glass counter front. Others are removing the food we've already laid out for the day, tipping it into trash bags.

"Hey!" I shout, jabbing a finger at them. "That's my product."

"Not anymore," Mr. Humphrey says in a bored tone. "It's a health and safety hazard and will be disposed of accordingly."

"Bullshit," I fume. "This is harassment. I'm calling the police, and I'll be suing every single one of you fuckers."

"Sorry, Nim," Sheriff Chancey says, appearing from the cats' rec room. That's where they sleep and also where all their carriers are stored. "I'm here to oversee the process on orders direct from the mayor. We can talk about it later. For now, I think we got all your kitties in there safely. One tried to slip out the door, but I caught her just in time."

"Fuck!" I exclaim. Chancey winces, but she gives me a sympathetic look.

"I'll go," Leah says, hauling the two cases in her hands with her. I trust her to make sure everyone's okay, so I wheel around to find Mrs. Durham huffing and puffing behind me.

"There's really no need for this, Mr. Decker," she says like I'm being completely unreasonable. "So much vulgar language."

"Language?" I repeat incredulously. "Fucking *language*? You come in here, terrorize already traumatized cats, harass me and my perfectly legal establishment, drive me out of business, and you have the audacity to get pissy about my mother-fucking potty mouth?"

"Please remain calm, Mr. Decker," she snips. "Everything happening here is all above board."

"Like fuck it is," I shoot back. "Your crooked husband will do anything to win this election for a town he does nothing for and where most of the people hate him."

I almost wish Jessie was here to witness how many words are coming out of my mouth. I don't think I've said this much all week.

But thinking of him brings a new layer of horror to the situation. My worst nightmare is coming true. I promised I'd provide for him like I did my employees and all my rescue kitties. And now one woman's vendetta and a fucked-up system of government is pulling it all down like a house of cards.

Mrs. Durham preens. "After today, Paddle Creek will be a thoroughly more respectable community, and the residents will be clamoring to thank my husband for all his hard work. You and your friends should have trusted in Jesus and led a more moral life. Then you all wouldn't be in this mess."

My blood runs cold.

I'm done talking to this bitch. I turn away from her just as Leah comes out of the back room and gives me two thumbs-up. Okay. The cats are safe. That's something.

But I have a feeling that the trouble is only just getting started.

First, I make sure that the tabby is still okay in my pocket. He's trembling, but he's stopped trying to make a break for it, so hopefully, that means he knows he's safe. Then I whip out my phone and call Donna over at O'Toole's. She answers after a couple of rings.

"Really not a good time, Nim," she snaps.

My heart sinks.

"Are they shutting you down, too?" I ask quietly.

There's a pause. "Mother-fucking *fuckers!*" she roars

before taking an audible breath and regaining some composure. "We need to reach out to the others. I'll call Candy. You got Ruben's number?"

I grunt and end the call, not wanting to waste any time. It's just turned seven, so I imagine neither the garage or the nail salon will be open. Like me, Donna lives above the pub. Our other friends might have nasty surprises waiting for them.

Or not. As it turns out, Durham didn't want to wait.

"Yeah," Ruben says in a horribly defeated voice. "They came banging on my door. Horowitz's has been classified as a crime scene, and the FBI is tearing it apart right now. The *FBI*, Nim. This started with reports of stolen cars and now they're insinuating that I've got ties with the *mafia.*"

I feel numb. How are we supposed to fight this when it's gotten to that level? Durham must know some really powerful people.

It's over. I look around as Humphrey shoves a manila envelope into my hands. I assume it has some kind of cease-and-desist order in it. I don't care. All the red tape stretched over my beloved café and the distressed faces of my employees tell me everything I need to know.

The tabby kitten pokes his head out and looks at me, giving me a sad little meow. He's got a dust bunny on him from his adventure on top of the fridge, so I carefully pluck it off him.

"Have a good day, Mr. Decker," Mrs. Durham says with vicious satisfaction. As she strides out of the café, her heels clip-clop on the tiles. Mr. Humphrey and his suited goons follow after her. The bell tinkles sadly as I watch them leave. Then I'm aware of just how quiet and still my beloved Toe Beans is.

"Nim," Leah says, taking a step forward.

"You should all go home," I say, unable to look any of

them in the eye. "I'll be in touch about taking care of the cats, but I'll handle it for today. I…I'm sorry."

"This isn't your fault," Leah starts to say hotly, but I'm ashamed to say I just turn away and walk into the rec room.

I sit down on the floor in the middle, where I'm surrounded by carriers, each with a scared little face looking out at me. There's a lump in my throat as I gently stroke the top of the tabby's head with a single finger.

I don't see any way back from this. Worse, I now have to go upstairs and wake Jessie so I can tell him what's happened before he goes to class. I promised him I wouldn't keep him in the dark anymore, and there's no way I'm letting him down again.

Not in that way, at least.

If I can't serve customers, how long can I feasibly hold on to Toe Beans? How fast will I have to close up shop? And after that, how long until I lose the apartment?

I know I need to face the music sooner rather than later. But just for now, I sit in the quiet with the cats I promised I would rehome and, in all likeliness, will now end up back at the shelter. I've let everybody down.

I knew I was a terrible Daddy.

CHAPTER 20

Jessie

Going to school after knowing what had happened to Toe Beans was almost impossible, but Nim insisted. I was so grateful that he hadn't shut me out from this devastating development that I trusted I could leave him, and we'd work on it when I got home after training later. But I won't lie. His hollow expression scared the shit out of me.

I could barely concentrate on Professor Knight's words, even though it was a really interesting philosophy class. But I was a love-sick kitten, and all I could think about was how I was going to try and save Nim. After all, he'd saved me. It was only fair.

What could I do, though? The mayor was obviously corrupt and had important people in his pocket. Nim was convinced that Sheriff Chancey was genuinely on our side, so if there was nothing she could do, then what hope did I have?

The DEA is investigating the pub. The FBI is at the garage. ICE is apparently rounding up all of the employees from the Butterflies salon for interrogation despite everyone being American citizens. Not to mention that O'Toole's isn't a brothel or drug den, and Horowitz's isn't illegally modi-fying stolen cars for the mafia.

Given that facts don't seem to matter to Mayor Durham, everyone is still understandably nervous.

How am I supposed to concentrate on what some president did a hundred years ago or what the subtext of a poem really means? My education is something that I chose to invest in because I knew my mom was out of the woods. But it's a luxury. It's not real life. What matters is *people*, not *grades*.

I'm not even excited to head to cheer practice, despite the fact that we've actually been getting better these past few training sessions. Cheerleading is my passion, but Tara and her cronies try so hard to suck the joy out of it some days I don't even know why I bother.

As I head over to the gym, I think about how I should just give Alannah my spot and walk away. But I realize that's my anxiety talking. We need to keep fighting until the day we're both competing side by side.

I didn't notice, but my mind was so preoccupied that I actually turned up to training late. Noticing at the last moment, I dash through the doors, my apologies at the ready, expecting to see everyone in full warm-up.

They're all sitting on the floor in a circle.

Some look sad. Some look mad. Tara looks smug, which is never a good sign.

One thing they all look at is me. I pause in my tracks. "Am I really that late?" I say, nervously checking my phone again.

Lakelyn stands up, a concerned expression on her face. She's holding a letter. Not a printout. An actual letter. I can see by the way it's been folded. "Jessie," she says. "I called the committee here early and I guess a few other people got the word, too. We've been discussing...well...I..."

"Jessie, it's *bullshit*," Alannah cries, jumping to her feet, her fists balled by her sides.

"Oh, calm down, Connick," Tara says with a snort, rolling her eyes.

Several of her friends laugh, but as I look around the circle, I realize the guy sitting next to her isn't one of the guys on the squad. He's got white-blond hair and a long face with sharp cheekbones. He'd probably be quite attractive if he wasn't sneering at me.

I don't recognize him, but he's holding Tara's hand, so I assume that's her rich boyfriend who she's always bragging about. Luke or something. What's he doing here?

Alannah comes to stand by my side, placing a reassuring hand on my back.

"Jessie, we have an issue," Lakelyn says, stopping in front of me and shaking her head.

She looks from the letter to Tara's boyfriend, and I get the feeling he might have brought it here. I'm not sure why it would have been hand-delivered instead of mailed, but that's the impression I get nonetheless.

"Honestly," Lakelyn continues, "I don't know what to make of it, and even less what we should do. But…someone has made a complaint against the squad. Against you."

After everything that's happened this morning, I'm immediately on high alert. "Me?" I say incredulously.

Lakelyn hands me the letter, but my vision is swimming too much to focus on it. "You know how for the Snowdown and all the Cheer First comps, we all have to sign that code of conduct to say that we're not involved in any kind of illegal activity…" She trails off.

My stomach drops. "No," I croak out.

"Since when are you in a biker gang, Garras?" Tara asks in mock concern.

"The only way he's getting in a biker gang is if he's the

pass-around party-bottom," her boyfriend says *just* loud enough for me to hear. The circle certainly hears, with about a third of them falling around laughing where they sit.

"Shut the fuck up, would you?" Zazzle snaps at him with a roll of her eyes.

My heart is racing, and my palms are sweaty as I turn back to Lakelyn. Her face is anxious, and she nods encouragingly, like I can say something to make this all better.

"M-my boyfriend," I stammer, trying to think of how I can possibly get out of this. "He's a biker, yeah. He has friends. They're in a chapter. The Cardinals. But…they just like riding motorcycles together, for crying out loud! None of that stuff anyone's saying is true!"

"What are they saying?" Lakelyn asks, her brows creasing.

I throw my hands up, finally losing the battle I've been having all day with my emotions. "That they're involved in drug dealing and prostitution and human trafficking and providing cars for the mafia! And that apparently my boyfriend's croissants are full of hairballs or something. It's ludicrous!"

"Then why are the feds at all those businesses checking for just that?" Tara's boyfriend asks, one eyebrow cocked like he's really got me.

"Because the mayor no doubt bribed some important people in order to help get his crooked ass reelected," I snap back.

Several people gasp. Alannah takes my hand and squeezes it.

"Jessie, this here is serious," Lakelyn says gently, taking the letter back from me.

"You don't have to tell me," I scoff.

I watch my captain smooth out the incriminating paper before looking back at me. "Whoever contacted Cheer First says they have solid evidence of your involvement with the gang. They say they won't go to the police…so long as you drop out of the competition."

"And the Kittens altogether," Tara chimes in with a nauseating smile. "We have to protect the whole squad, you see?"

Lakelyn shoots her a glare. "We never said anything like that. Stay out of this, Tara, and let me handle it."

My head is spinning. The *police?* Am I going to jail?

"Jessie's done nothing wrong," Alannah hisses. "Neither has Nim. This is completely fabricated. What are they even claiming he's done?"

Lakelyn looks at me so sadly. "It says they have someone willing to testify that you…bought drugs."

"Jessie would never—" Alannah yells.

I place my hand on her chest. The look on my face is enough to get her to stop talking.

My mom would have qualified for her med card, but the dispensaries weren't open yet, and she was in so much pain. It was just a little weed. But I went to that dealer several times. If someone found him…

"I'll resign from the squad," I say quietly.

"Jessie, no," Alannah rasps.

"We can fight this," Lakelyn tells me tearfully. "You belong here, Jessie. You've breathed life into this team."

Tara scoffs, but at least has the good grace not to say anything.

I shake my head. "I don't want you to fight and risk the whole team getting banned," I say truthfully. "I don't want to cause any trouble. I never did. I just wanted to cheer. I can give you back the hoodie if you need me to."

I only got it last week, and I've been living in it ever since. But I never even got my competition uniform. All we need for games is the Kittens T-shirt.

I guess that's my cheer career over. I'll never get to step on a competition mat ever again. All those years of hoping and dreaming that I could get back to who I was before cancer reared its ugly head…for nothing.

Well, not for nothing. I don't regret or resent a single second I spent with my mom. I certainly don't regret coloring outside of the lines to get something that would have been perfectly legal if the dispensaries were open in order to stop her from crying and vomiting from the pain she was in.

But I am sad. For me, for Nim, for everyone this ugly business has dragged into the mud.

"The hoodie is yours. Of course it is," Lakelyn says, visibly distressed. "The suspension is just for this competition. I'll sort it out, I promise. We want you to stay."

"Actually," Tara says, sounding angry for the first time. It's funny, but I appreciate her genuine emotion rather than the fake niceties she usually panders us with. "I don't want him to stay. I never wanted him or his trashy friend on the squad at all, let alone being allowed to represent us on the competition mat."

"Tara," Lakelyn says, sounding like she's begging her to stop. "Have some fucking empathy."

Tara folds her arms as her boyfriend gets to his feet, smoothing down his blazer. Everyone else here is dressed for a workout, and he looks like he's off to a country club.

He probably is.

"I know," Tara says. "Why don't we put it to a vote? Those who want the little criminal Jessie to stay on our team and risk us getting banned from competitions for the rest of the year—maybe forever—raise your hand."

Alannah shoves her hand straight up into the air. So do the other members of my stunt group, Zazzle, and a couple more girls who are shooting daggers at Tara. A lot of people look worriedly anywhere but me. I don't blame them. They're thinking of the squad, and they should be. But

Tara's friends around her grin and wave good-bye in my direction.

"No, I'm not voting," Lakelyn says stubbornly. "It's not that simple. I can fix this. Y'all have just got to give me time. Brittany's aunt is the sheriff. I'm sure we can talk to her and—"

I cut her off by wrapping my arms around her. "It's okay," I say. "This isn't your fault. I don't blame you for one second. But the team comes first. That's what cheerleading is all about. I'll miss you all."

She hugs me back tightly. When I let her go, she has tears in her eyes. She looks at me for a few long moments before giving the smallest nod. "Don't be a stranger," she whispers.

"I promise, I won't," I tell her.

I nod toward the rest of the squad, a lot of whom wave sadly. Then at Alannah.

"Give 'em hell," I murmur quietly. Then I have to march myself out the door unless I want to run the risk of crying in front of Tara, and I'd never give her the satisfaction.

I don't make it three feet outside before a body crashes into me, their arms trying to squeeze me in half. "Sorry," Alannah says breathlessly. "I had to grab my stuff and give Tara the bird before I could run after you."

"Wha-?" I utter, turning in her grip.

She scowls at me. "You didn't seriously think I wasn't going to quit as well, do you?" She boops my nose. "Come on. Let's go back to my room and get *seriously* drunk and listen to some very loud Avril Lavigne."

I laugh, but it turns into a sob. "I love you," I mumble as I throw my arms around her neck.

"I know, kitten," she says softly. "It's going to be okay."

I'm not sure about that. But I am very sure about cheap vodka and some seriously obnoxious 00s punk pop.

At some point, I would have to tell Nim. But his heart is

broken enough for one day. My shitty news could wait until tomorrow, especially if I get so wasted that I passed out in Alannah's bed, which is my current plan of action.

This was the worst day ever. But at least when you're at rock bottom, the only way is up.

Right?

CHAPTER 21
Nim

I'M NOT REALLY SURE HOW I'M GOING TO GET THROUGH THE day. Keeping busy seems the best option. So after I manage to shake myself from my catatonic state, I set about thoroughly washing every single litter box and food dish both in the café and my apartment. Since we are most definitely closed, I drop all the blinds in Toe Beans and open up the carriers. Slowly, the cats start creeping out to investigate what's going on.

I wish I could explain it to them, but I don't really know myself.

Once I've cleaned their stuff, I tackle the café. Those bastards didn't care what a mess they made as they tossed all my food, so there are crumbs and sticky smears all over the counter area. Then I wash the inside of the windows. Because why not?

By mid-afternoon the cats are mostly out in the café again, so I take some time to groom them. The long-haired breeds get brushed every single day, but the short-hairs enjoy the sensation as well. Or at least, it's good for them. Some try to wriggle away, but I'm able to wrangle them long enough to tend to most of their backs and tails. After the day I've had, I skip most of their bellies. It's not worth the stress for anyone.

It's around this time that Jessie texts me to let me know that he's with his friend Alannah and that he won't be back until later so not to worry about dinner. I won't lie, not only does that worry me but it also stings slightly. If there was ever a day I needed to hug my boy, it's today. But then he texts once more saying he's staying overnight with her and again there's no explanation given as to why. I start to worry that something might actually be wrong.

I don't sleep well. It's not the first night we've spent apart since we got together as he's crashed with Alannah before. But my bed is still very empty, and my head is very full. So I toss and turn into the early hours of the morning, pissing off my cats until I finally pass out.

It's incredibly strange not setting my alarm for five o'clock, and also pointless as I wake up early anyway. I will myself to try and get some more rest, but eventually I give in and go and put some coffee on. I told my staff that I'd message them, but I haven't yet. So I stick to taking care of all the cats for the time being as it keeps me preoccupied.

Jessie is really concerning me, now.

In the end, he comes walking through the back entrance of the café at around ten-ish looking bedraggled. I rush to him right away, and throw my arms around him. "You okay?" I grunt.

"There was vodka," he says, his voice hoarse. "So much vodka."

I stroke his hair and kiss his forehead. "Breakfast?" I've got bacon, eggs, hashbrowns, pancakes, whatever he wants.

"Maybe in a bit," he says with a sigh. "Alannah did already force a PBJ down me as well as heavily sugared coffee."

I take his hand and lead him to sit on one of the sofas. It's so odd to see the place unoccupied in the morning daylight, but I push those thoughts aside for now. Something is definitely not right with my kitten.

"What's wrong?" I ask bluntly. I used all my words on Mrs. Durham yesterday, but the ones I have spare you bet I'm going to dredge up for Jessie.

He huffs, and his shoulders sag before he crawls into my lap, his legs draped over my thighs and his arms around my neck. "It's stupid compared to your problems. I don't mean to be this upset. It's just…well, it's a lot after the past few years, you know? And I didn't see it coming at *all*. Because it's such fucking bullshit and…"

He sighs and takes a deep breath, the soft puff hitting my skin. I stroke his back. "Your problems aren't stupid," I assure him.

It's not the suffering Olympics. Whatever has made him feel this way is valid. Has someone been mean to him? I don't care if they're a college kid. I shall be using my full, scary intimidation tactics that I reserve for special occasions.

"You could lose your business and your home," Jessie says. "This is just…petty. I'll be fine."

I can't lie. It stings that he says it's my home and not ours. Doesn't he think of it that way? Has he been considering moving somewhere else this whole time?

That's not the point. I'm so low it's making me insecure, like when I was a teenager and I'd lash out because I was so angry and brutally hurt. That's when I learned it was much better not to speak at all or at least consider my words very carefully so I wouldn't accidentally inflict more harm on others.

"Kitten," I say, using my firm Daddy voice.

He sighs again and lifts his head to look at me. His eyes are red-rimmed either from the hangover or…or he's been crying that much.

"I had to quit the team."

Of all the things I was expecting him to say, that was not on the list. "What?" I cry. "Why?"

He shrugs and looks away. My heart is racing. I don't understand. Cheerleading is his *life*.

"They made you leave?" I try again.

"It was what was best for the team," he says hollowly.

"How?" I demand. "Jessie, what's going on?"

He nibbles his lip and gives me a shifty look. "Promise you won't freak out?"

What kind of a question is that? We are so far past freaking out already. "No."

He huffs. "Nim, I'm serious! This is just something that's happened, and it's not…it's not your fault, okay?"

Ice rushes through my veins. My fault? "What happened?" I press again, my throat tight and my skin hot. Perhaps that's why he said 'your' home and not 'our'? He already knows I've fucked him over and that I can't protect or provide for him. I made a promise, and I broke it.

This is why he's so upset.

Whatever's happened *is* my fault.

A tear tumbles down his cheek, and I immediately brush it away with my thumb. *Fuck.* I love him so much. Leah's right. I should tell him. But if I've hurt him this badly, then do I really have that right in this moment?

He takes a shuddery breath, looking utterly wretched. "Competitions have these moral codes to promote healthy, happy lifestyles, blah blah blah. As long as you're not a dick about it, people don't really care. But if the cheerleading organizations are informed about a team breaking the rules, they're legally obliged to deal with it."

"What kinds of rules?" I ask, dread sitting heavily on my chest.

I already know what he's going to say.

"Someone told Cheer First that…that I'm in a violent gang and involved with drugs."

All the blood drains from my head. If I wasn't sitting down then I would have been very abruptly. "This *is* my fault," I utter.

"No, Nim, please," Jessie says, waving his hands. "It's really not. They say this guy has given a witness statement from back home. He's telling them I bought drugs, and it's basically true, but it's not what you think, I swear! It was for my mom! The other stuff is just bullshit like we know it is for you and Candy and everyone else. Tara's boyfriend was there, and I think maybe he has something to do with the mayor. It's just stupid smear politics and propaganda and all that. Nim, are you listening to me?"

I'm really not.

They've gone after Jessie to punish me. To make sure I understand it's not just me who's fucked—like I wasn't already aware of that anyway. This is the dream that's been fueling him through all the harrowing years his mom fought against cancer. It's in his blood, who he is.

And those bastards have taken it away.

Not on my watch.

I promised I would do everything in my power to protect him and do what's right for him.

Even if that breaks my heart.

"You're not in any gang," I say, untangling myself from him. He reaches for me, but I stand up, folding my arms and leaning against a nearby table. "They can't kick you out."

"Technically, I quit," Jessie says hotly. "You're not listening. That's not the point. The weed thing *is* true. I refuse to drag the whole team down. It was a choice I made, and I can't take it back. It's not fair, but I'm not going to destroy the whole cheerleading program just because of that!"

I shake my head. "It's my fault. If you distance yourself

from me, you can go back and tell them it was all a misunderstanding. They'll have to take you back."

He stares at me until it gets uncomfortable. "What do you mean 'distance' myself?" he asks, his voice dangerously low.

"I won't ruin your life, Jessie," I growl, unable to look at him, so I focus on a gray cat that's come to sit by my feet, her tail swishing. She can feel the tension.

I can't blame her.

Jessie's voice is wobbly when he speaks. "Are you breaking up with me?" he whispers.

I grind my teeth, my anger toward the Durhams so powerful I'm surprised it isn't shooting through the walls like a laser beam in the direction of their ghastly mansion. There is no reason that they're doing this other than because they want to. Because they can.

But the way I see it is this is an impossible situation and I have to do what's best for Jessie, even if he can't see it.

"I'll go speak to the dean or whatever. Tell them you're just my tenant. They don't have any grounds to keep you off the team. Not if it's just word of mouth."

He springs to his feet, tears spilling down his face. It's the most awful thing I've ever seen. "Nim! What the fuck? Stop this right now! The cheer thing is over, done. It wasn't your fault, and you dumping me will only break my heart!"

I shake my head. "I knew I was no good for you. You've got your whole life ahead of you, Jessie. I won't ruin it. You can stay, obviously. But I'll keep my distance. Be respectful."

"You are doing the *opposite* of respecting me right now, Benjamin Decker!" he yells, anger flashing over his features. I wince as if he'd struck me across the face. "I *chose* to walk away from the squad to avoid scandal, and I'm *choosing* to be with you! I'm an adult, and I know what I want! Please —*please* listen to me!"

I cling to the table to stop my hands from shaking. I want

to keep him more than anything in the world. More than my home or my business, I want *him*.

But that's selfish. I have to do what's best for him.

"I can't," I say.

It's like I can feel my heart crack in two as I push myself off the table and walk away.

CHAPTER 22

Jessie

"HE'S A STUPID…STUPID…*STUPID* HEAD," ALANNAH SAYS OVER the loud music with a scowl.

I sigh and sip my cocktail, and I can't say I disagree with her.

Despite last night's antics and the ensuing hangover today, after Nim's enraging behavior this morning, I've found myself dragged out tonight to The Ice Cream Parlor to drown my sorrows for a second evening in a row. The fifties diner vibe is cheerful, I'll admit. Everything is minty green with red leather seats and neon lights. But it's going to take a whole lot more than a fun bar to lift my spirits.

I was a fool for thinking things couldn't get much worse yesterday.

Part of me knows that Nim is hurting and afraid. He truly believes that by pushing me away he can protect me. The other part of me knows that he's a *stupid head* that is going to feel very *stupid* once he pulls his stupid head out of his *ass*.

If. *If* he pulls his head out of his ass.

I'm not giving up on us just yet, but I also have my

dignity. If he genuinely doesn't want to be with me anymore, I'm not going to beg.

The thought that our relationship could really be over makes me choke down a sob. Alannah rubs my back and gives me a pitiful look. We're perched on stools around a small table while the resident drag queen, Kimmi Sugar, lip-syncs the shit out of a Beyoncé song. The bar is reasonably busy—enough to allow me to feel like I can get lost in the crowd.

Oh, god. I love that useless man. And I never got to tell him.

Why wouldn't he talk to me or even listen to what I was saying? The situation with the cheer squad is totally shit, but I can come to terms with it in time, I'm sure.

I'm never going to forgive Nim if he blows up what we have because he's too stubborn to believe that he's actually a good person who has *not* ruined my life. Because leaving me *will* ruin my life.

Stupid head.

Alannah knocks back the last of her cocktail. It's happy hour so they're two-for-one, and we're making the most of it. "More drinks!" she cries, hopping off her stool to head back to the bar.

I'm so grateful she's my bestie. Everyone should have someone so loyal and fierce by their side when their Daddy has a wobble and…well I don't even know how to sum up what's happening with the cheer squad. When someone uses you as a pawn in a mass political conspiracy, perhaps? Fuck, when did my life become so complicated?

"Fancy seeing you here," a smooth voice drawls. I turn around and see a familiar face grinning at me.

"Kadence!" I cry, throwing my arms around his neck. I teeter on the stool but manage not to slip off it, thankfully.

Okay, so maybe I've had a few more porn star martinis than I was aware.

But he hugs me back and kisses my cheek before he settles me back down and lets me go. I notice he's with that same slim, tall blond guy from the library. "Jessie, this is my friend Harper. He's an amazing artist. Harper, this is Jessie. He's a kitten."

He waggles his eyebrows, but my heart sinks. "Not anymore," I say glumly. "I had to leave the squad because the mayor hates me."

Kadence blinks and looks thoroughly confused. "Oh! You're talking about cheerleading. I was talking about kink. Wait, what? The mayor? You had to leave the squad?"

I let out a strangled noise and cover my eyes. "Oh, *that* kind of kitten! I guess I'm still one of those, even though my Daddy might not be my Daddy anymore. *Stupid* Daddy."

Tears pool in my eyes again, but I can still see Kadence and Harper share a concerned look before pulling up a couple of spare stools to sit down with me and placing their drinks on our table. "Did you break up with your Daddy?" Harper asks, sounding genuinely sorry for me.

"Oh, yeah," I say, tilting my head as I look at him. "You have three Daddies, right? That's crazy but so, so cool."

Harper gives me a fond look. I get the feeling the two of them haven't had as many cocktails as me. "Technically, I have a Daddy wolf, a Papa wolf, and a Baby wolf," he says.

"And he's the little lamb," Kadence says, tickling Harper's side. Harper bats him away, but they're both grinning. That's right. Kadence said something about Harper getting chased...

"We were talking about you, though," Harper says gently. "Are you okay?"

I shrug. "Some bad stuff happened that wasn't my Daddy's fault, but he's determined to take the blame anyway.

He says he's 'protecting me.'" I use air quotes to show what I think of that nonsense. "Oh, hey!" I cry as Alannah comes back with our drinks. "This is my bestie, Alannah! Alannah, this is Kadence and Harper. They're kinky Daddy's boys, too." As soon as the words come out of my mouth, I slap my hand over it. "I'm so sorry," I mumble through my fingers. "I didn't mean to say that out loud."

Luckily, both of them laugh before shaking hands with Alannah after she sits down.

"Don't worry about it," Kadence assures me. "We're pretty open about it with other kinksters. Now let's get back to your Daddy. What's going on? Didn't he like the new gear?"

"Oh, no," I say, shaking my head vigorously. "He *loved* it. That's not the problem."

Between the two of us, we explain the whole messed up situation with the mayor. But we quickly realize that they know a lot of it already because Harper's Papa actually works at Horowitz's and is a Cardinal biker, too. In fact, he reckons that's probably why the garage is being targeted like it is.

"It's all just such bullshit!" Alannah bemoans. The drag queen is taking a break, so the regular music is playing again, and it's not quite as loud, so we don't have to shout so much.

"Agreed," Kadence says, and they clink their glasses together. "I don't know what you can do about all of..." He waves his hand around in a circular motion. "...that. But surely your Daddy can be made to see reason. Have you tried talking to him again?"

I shake my head. "He went out on his bike. He hadn't come back before Alannah dragged me out. I might stay with her again tonight. I don't want to go back drunk and tell him he's a stupid head. Because he's not really."

"He is right now," Alannah grumbles.

Harper rests his hand over mine. "It sounds to me like you've still got everything to fight for," he tells me sincerely.

"Relationships are hard, believe me. I'm still finding my feet with mine. But…do you love him?"

I swallow and glance at Alannah, who gives me a supportive smile. "Yeah, I'm pretty sure I do," I say.

He pats my hand. "When you go back home, you just tell him that. Don't take no for an answer. Make him realize he's worth fighting for because he might not think he is."

"He doesn't," I agree sadly. "Which is crazy because he's amazing."

"He sounds it," Harper says. "But so are you. Don't forget that." I know we've only just met properly, but the validation makes me feel all warm and fuzzy.

Kadence huffs. "See, this is why I just stick to fucking. Emotions are so *complicated.*" We all laugh, but he wraps an arm around my back. "I am with Harper, though. I still think you've got everything to play for. It's not over until the fat lady sings."

"Cheers to that," Alannah declares, raising her glass. We all copy her, coming together in the middle to tap drinks without spilling any.

I raise it to my lips to take a sip…and end up spitting it over the table instead. "Lakelyn?" I cry as I hastily wipe my chin. "What the hell are you all doing here?"

The others turn around to see my cheer captain rushing up to our table. By her side are Zazzle and Brittany, and they all look slightly flustered but excited. I was barely aware of who Brittany was until yesterday, so I'm definitely not sure of what she's doing here.

"Alannah told us where y'all were, so we jumped on the tram," Lakelyn explains.

Alannah frowns. "I did? Oh, yeah! I did!" She leans over to me and tries to whisper over the music. "They texted when I was at the bar. I told her to come here and apologize." She crinkles her nose and giggles.

"Oh, no, you didn't have to do that," I say, feeling bad.

"It sounds like they do to me," Kadence mumbles into his drink.

Lakelyn shakes her head. "We were blindsided yesterday, Jessie. That letter was threatening the whole squad with legal action and being banned by Cheer First. I know you were just trying to protect us, but I never wanted you to leave."

It suddenly strikes me that the language she's using is *exactly* what I've been saying to Nim. I open and close my mouth, but nothing comes out.

"Well, it's too little too late," Alannah says firmly.

Lakelyn gives her a sad smile. "I know that. But we never wanted you to leave either, hon. In fact, I think your loyalty to Jessie is fucking admirable."

It's Alannah's turn to open and close her mouth. "Thank you," she says eventually.

Zazzle rests her hand on Lakelyn's shoulder. "The reason why we're here is that this is—as Alannah rightly said yesterday—all bullshit. We're not going to take it lying down."

"No, we're not!" Lakelyn agrees excitedly. "I told you Brittany here is the niece of the sheriff, right?" Brittany gives us all a wave, but unfortunately, I don't find this information to be as inspiring as Lakelyn perhaps hopes.

"Sorry, El," I say, giving her what I hope is an earnest look. "Sheriff Chancey was literally there when the mayor's wife stormed into the café and shut it down. She was keeping the peace and helping my boyfriend, but she was also told directly by the mayor to enforce his decision."

But the girls are all shaking their heads. "This isn't about my aunt, actually," Brittany says. "Not technically. We can explain everything. In fact, I can show you right now if you want?" She swings her backpack around and gets her laptop halfway out before raising her eyebrows.

I blink in surprise. We only have a little table, but I'm definitely intrigued. I look around at the others.

"Oh, I definitely need to see this," Alannah says.

"If we're going to work on battle plans," Kadence declares, "Harper and I need refills. Ladies?"

"I'll come with you," Zazzle offers.

Harper starts making as much space as possible on the table. Lakelyn spots a nearby unoccupied one and drags it over to place it next to our existing one.

There's a flutter in my chest. For the first time since yesterday morning, something like hope dances in my heart. I'm not sure if it's naïve to think I can do anything to get myself back on the squad, but there's a feeling of defiance in the air between this eclectic group of people that makes me feel stronger.

I wish Nim was here. But maybe I need to tackle his concerns from a different angle before I can go back to him and try and make him see sense. Perhaps whatever the cheer girls want to show me will help give me a new perspective. Right now, this feels like exactly where I need to be.

For more than one reason.

I tell the group I'm going to nip to the bathroom before we get settled in, so I hop down from the table.

And come face-to-face with Parker.

My breath hitches, and I take a step backward, bumping into the table. I feel rather than see my friends all look up.

"Parker?" I say in surprise. His actual boyfriend, who I've already forgotten the name of is standing by his side. I guess they didn't break up after all.

I thought I would be angry about that. I thought I'd feel a lot of things at seeing my ex again. I've daydreamed a great deal about this moment and always imagined it with Nim by my side so that I could prove to Parker how much I'd moved on from him and how much of an upgrade I'd made.

Except Nim isn't here. We might not even still be together.

And yet I find myself looking at this weak, pathetic little man who never treated me right, and still manage to stand tall. Things might be complicated with Nim in this precise moment, but everything he's done for me until now has made me feel treasured and so very important.

"Who's Parker?" Kadence asks loudly, carrying a tray of drinks and shots back to our tables. "Do we like Parker?"

"Parker is the mouth-breather who made Jessie think they were dating when Jessie was his bit on the side the whole time," Alannah says even louder.

I glance back and see six people square up, murderous looks on their faces. I turn back in time to see Parker's boyfriend wince.

Yeah, dude. You chose to stay. It might not hurt you to get a reminder of who you're really sharing a bed with.

"Y-you look good," Parker says to me.

"Thank you," I say genuinely with a smile.

I think the old me would have automatically repeated the compliment back, but he doesn't deserve that. He treated me like an absolute fool. Instead, I play just the tiniest bit dirty.

"I didn't think you knew about Creams?" I ask Parker innocently. "You never brought me here."

This time, his boyfriend takes a step away from him, looking him up and down.

Okay, that's good enough for me. I actually don't care what he thinks anymore—of me or anything else. That in itself is a revelation. Who'd have known that indifference was empowering?

"Well, I hope you guys have a good night," I tell them sincerely. I doubt it'll happen now, but that's not my problem. "My friends and I have some things we need to talk about."

"And alcohol to drink," Alannah adds.

"And dicks to suck!" Kadence chimes in with two thumbs-up. "You guys have fun. I bet you're going to have *great* sex tonight!"

Without a word, Parker and his boyfriend turn and melt into the crowd and don't look back.

Someone whistles behind me. Someone else comments that in this case, karma is like a kitten, making me think of Leah.

I take a deep breath. I know everything else is still royally fucked up, and my relationship with Nim is far from stable. But after that little encounter, I can't help but feel stronger. Taller. Ready for a fight. I'm not sure with who—Tara, the mayor, or the god damned FBI—but the point is that I've decided I'm not just going to lie down and take it.

I am not alone. My mom and I have beaten something far scarier than this.

Bring it on.

CHAPTER 23

Nim

"THIS IS NEVER GOING TO WORK," I SAY, FULLY AWARE I'M being defeatist and annoying, and yet apparently unable to stop myself anyway.

"Have you got any better ideas?" Donna asks. She knows I don't, so I just grunt and get off the back of my bike, kick the stand and open up the lock box to put my helmet inside. I see the one Jessie borrowed. and anguish lances through me so fast and hard I think I may pass out.

No matter how much I tell myself I've done the right thing, it's still hurting like a motherfucker. Causing my baby boy pain was something I wanted to avoid at all costs. But this shitstorm doesn't seem to be blowing over anytime soon, and I know his first competition is only a few weeks away. If he's got any chance of pulling his reputation—his *life*—back together, I can't be anywhere near him.

But I know there's a reason why I haven't admitted to Donna what I've done. Part of me knows that pushing him away like that was cruel. Sometimes, though, you have to be cruel to be kind.

I can't think about that now. Otherwise, I'll be no good to

anyone. So I secure my lockbox and follow Donna. There's a group of people up ahead handing out signs on wooden sticks. Others have made their own.

The idea of holding something in my hands makes me feel itchy. I plan on just standing around being intimidating. That's always worked for me in the past.

It turns out that Mayor Durham and his wife might have a house that's hidden behind a gate, but their street sure doesn't have any kind of barriers beyond that. So the Cardinals have decided to have a little get-together out here. That's our right, after all. We're not breaking any laws.

Maybe it's time these awful people feel what it's like to be harassed. Except, unlike us, they will have one hundred percent earned it.

I'm quite impressed. There are already around thirty to forty people gathered. I see bikers I know from rides and the pub. But also employees from the garage and the nail salon as well as what I guess are friends and family of those who have been specifically targeted.

Seeing all this support makes me feel less like I'm drowning all by myself. I'm not sure it can possibly change anything, but it beats sitting at home alone, worrying about anything and everything. Maybe down the line, we'll be able to prove that all these accusations were completely false, so it might be that the only thing that can save our businesses will be word of mouth.

It's worth a shot, at least.

"Where do you want me, boss?" Leah asks as she bounds up to me. She was pretty miffed at me for going radio silent on her. But as soon as I let her know that Donna was organizing this rally, she perked right up to her usual bubblegum self again. By her side is a Black girl with short blonde hair and numerous piercings. I haven't seen her before, but I wonder if this is the 'not a date' girl Leah mentioned. I'm happy for her if she's made a new friend.

Some of my employees are setting up a water and snack station to make sure no one gets dehydrated or low on blood sugar. Leah's got her phone out, ready to live-stream us across Instagram. It won't be the first time we've used our fifty thousand-plus subscribers for a socio-political cause. They might have started following us for daily cute kitty action, but they also know how to rally when called upon.

I'm really hoping that we can perhaps get some momentum going for support online. That *might* just pressure the mayor to call off his hate campaign. It's probably too little too late, but I just can't stand the idea of him winning like this. That's the way the world works, though, isn't it? Those with power often get it by trampling on others to reach the top. If we can try and make some of the wider world see what a crook he's been, maybe that will be some kind of justice.

God knows we almost certainly won't get any real recompense.

"All right, everyone!" Donna yells, clapping her hands before waving people closer to her. "We're here to make some noise. We'll be doing some filming so we can spread the word, but we do want to get the attention of our dear mayor and his lovely wife as well. So don't do anything *stupid* now. No throwing shit over the gate. Try and keep your language PG-13 so we don't give them an excuse to censor us. Keep your tempers in check. Sound good?"

The crowd claps and shouts back various affirmations. I see Ruben, the owner of Horowitz's, standing with his arms around his boy, Xander. He's got a picture of a T-rex on his poster that reads 'EAT THE RICH,' which makes me smile.

"We've got a few live-streams going," Donna continues, "but just ignore them. The folks directing them know what they're doing, and if they need anything in particular from you, they'll holler. Now, we've got some chants we want to do, but they're super easy, so don't worry. And…uh…"

She frowns, her words trailing off as she squints down the road. My heart flips, worrying that it's the sheriff come to shut us down before we've even begun. But it's not a cop car that Donna's focusing on.

It's a group of people walking along the street. And they're wearing a lot of purple and teal.

My heart leaps into my throat as I realize now that our throng has gone quiet that I can hear the newcomers yelling a chant of their own, and there's a beat banging out on drums. They're on both sides of the residential street, flanking a car that's rolling slowly toward us. No—there are several cars, I think. As they approach, their voices are becoming louder and louder, and I can see people jumping and dancing around excitedly.

And leading them is a young man wearing cat ears.

I gasp as my hand flies in front of my mouth. It can't be, can it?

Really, I should have learned by now not to underestimate my boy.

"What's going on?" Leah asks me. She's got her phone up, streaming everything live for our channel. I can see how crazy the comments are going.

"I think the cavalry just arrived," I say faintly.

It's not just cheerleaders who are with Jessie—which—I don't understand? I thought he had to quit the squad? Anyway, I can also see football players and members of the marching band—that would explain the drums. Also plenty of people in regular clothing. God, there's got to be at least a hundred of them, surely?

As they get closer, I can see they're also filming themselves as well as us. The cheerleaders are leading the charge at the front, as their name might suggest, shaking pom-poms and clapping. Other people have signs similar to ours, calling the mayor a liar and demanding justice. Several signs are asking to see the receipts. I don't really know what that means, but I'm guessing they're on our side.

"Hey, there," Donna says, stepping forward with a wave. "Have you come to join us?"

A small Asian girl skips forward to shake her hand. She's wearing a cheerleading uniform and has teal glitter on her eyelids, sparkling in the sunlight. "We have!" she cries. "I'm Lakelyn, the captain of the Paddle Creek Kittens. We brought some friends with us. I hope that's okay?"

"Girl, the more, the merrier," Donna says. Her brow is slightly creased. "But, uh, why?"

The captain glances back at Jessie before turning back to Donna. "We heard there were folks who needed help, and that's what we do, ma'am. Besides, we came across some information we thought might help y'all."

Jessie purposefully hasn't met my eye yet, but my attention is pulled from him as I see cheerleaders starting to make their way into the crowd, handing out leaflets. I take one with a frown. "What's this?" I ask the girl with purple in her long braids who gave it to me.

She winks. "Oh, nothing you can't find all over the internet…as of about three hours ago."

With a cackle, she keeps moving through the throng. I glance down at the leaflet.

My first impression is that there are a lot of statistics and a few photos. I recognize Mayor Durham right away. He seems to be standing next to or shaking hands with various different people. Someone near me gasps. Another voice whoops, and I see people start to excitedly chatter to each other. I'm struggling to focus on the information right now, but it seems to be talking about all the people Durham bribed in order to get our businesses shut down. Not to mention clearly outlining his embezzlement charges.

Whoa.

Hope blossoms in my chest like a fragile little flower. Where did they find all this dirt? Could this actually make a difference? Sway the community if we spread what really happened backed up by facts? I know not everyone cares about the truth when they're whipped up into a frenzy, but it might be enough to get some people to switch their votes to Sanchez instead.

I have to discuss everything with my favorite person, the one who I think made this all happen. When I look up, though, Jessie has vanished. My heart drops. All I want to do is run to him, gather him up in my arms, and never let him go. But he might not want that. I wouldn't blame him if he were furious with me.

As I anxiously scan the crowd, he's nowhere to be found. The drums and whistles are so loud now I feel like I'm at the football stadium. Speaking of which, I spy an assistant coach I've seen at some of the games. He's with Trey, one of the guys who works at the garage with Ruben. He seems to pull his bike apart more than he rides it, but I know him and his husband from the pub. The football coach is their boyfriend. So is the slim, young blond guy with them.

Leah is still filming, but she's been joined by that gothy woman who came into the café, asking about a new black cat —the mama Leah apparently helped to find around the back of the library at the college. She and the other blonde girl seem mesmerized by the pale woman, who I think is the librarian. She's talking to the assistant coach. Next to the other blonde girl is a man rocking a tennis skirt confidently holding hands with an older man in a tweed suit. Oh—it's Mr. British Reusable Cup.

The cars have parked around us and are blocking the

street. I see more customers I recognize from the café. People have come out wearing uniforms from not only Butterflies but also the garden center, the convenience store, the Sunken Treasure motel, and that cheesy dinosaur fast food place, Dino-Mite.

That drag queen from The Ice Cream Parlor who did the bingo night at O'Toole's is dressed to impress from the top of her enormous purple wig to the tip of her six-inch sparkling heels. She's with a woman in a uniform from the tram company, writing signs on cardboard, using the hood of a car for support.

I realize it's not just any car. It's Sheriff Chancey's. As I catch her eye, she waves at me, her two teens by her side looking surprisingly enthusiastic. The boy is filming, narrating what's going on for his followers. The girl...well, she looks delighted by the events unfurling around her. And their mom has her hands on both their shoulders, looking proud.

Community. That's what I see. A network of people who care about this damn town despite the fact that its own mayor doesn't. Not for the first time I wonder why he wants the job in the first place. It's certainly not to do it well. Some men just want to be on the top of the pile even if it's made from broken pieces, I guess.

I feel a tap on my arm, so I look around.

And there he is.

"Jessie," I say, my heart leaping into my mouth. God, he looks gorgeous despite having crashed in his best friend's room for the past couple of days. I hated that he never came home. I can't stand what I did to him.

He takes a deep breath. "Stupid head," he says, folding his arms and scowling at me.

"Uh...yeah. I deserve that." I feel awkward as I turn the leaflet around in my hands. "Did you do this?"

He shrugs. "It was a team effort. Turns out one of the girls has a cousin who's like a whiz hacker. The captain came and found me to tell me that she never wanted me to leave the squad. But it wasn't just about me. It's bigger than that."

We both look at the crowd around us, all yelling and waving their banners. A couple of security guards have come down to glare at us from the other side of the gate, but for now, they aren't doing anything more than that. Considering the sheriff is already here making sure we keep the peace, there isn't much more they *can* do as I see it.

A TV crew has arrived. It feels like every other person has their phones out, filming events as they occur. The cheer captain has a group interviewing her as she talks them through the accusations against Mayor Durham and his wife.

It *is* bigger than just us, but honestly in that moment, Jessie is all I care about.

"Are you okay?" I ask.

He nibbles his lower lip. "Not really," he mumbles. "I told you not to break my heart, and you did it anyway. And before you say it," he says, holding up his hand as I open my mouth to protest, "I know you think you were protecting me. I know you think that you're bad for my image and that my life would have been just peachy without you. But you're wrong, okay? I'm so sorry your family made you think that way about yourself. What they did to you was unforgivable. But that was a long time ago, Nim. If you don't start accepting that people love you and want you in their lives now, you might be too afraid to ever do it."

I'm aware that my jaw is hanging open. My heart is racing, and a shiver runs over my skin.

"Love?" I utter. I don't deserve that word, but I want it anyway.

He rolls his eyes, a hint of a smile playing on his lips. "Yes, stupid head. I love you, okay? But if you don't want to be with me—"

I don't give him a chance to finish. I grab him and pull him into a crushing hug, inhaling his scent as I bury my nose into his hair, loving how his fluffy cat ear tickles my cheek.

"I love you too, Kitten," I say thickly. "So much. I was trying to be strong and do what was right for you, but I can see how wrong I was now. You're everything to me. I only ever wanted your happiness, and if you'll let me be a part of that, I'll never take it for granted again."

He leans back with a laugh, his eyes wet from tears. "Whoa, there, cowboy. Slow down before you hurt yourself. That was a terrifying number of words from you."

I grunt out a laugh and brush a lock of hair back from his forehead. "That's been happening a lot lately. I guess it's easier to talk when I really care about something. Or someone." We look into each other's eyes for a moment, and my heart finally feels like it's beating properly again for the first time in days. "May I kiss you?"

"You can kiss me forever, Daddy," he says, leaning into me.

His lips taste like heaven, and his body fits perfectly in my arms. It's funny he mentioned forever, because that's where I want him to stay until the end of time.

"I hope you can forgive me," I mumble into his mouth.

"Already forgiven," he mumbles back.

"Jessie! Oh, hey…uh…"

We pull apart, and I see a redheaded girl with a pixie cut looking awkwardly at us. From descriptions I've heard, I guess this must be Alannah.

"I guess you guys made up," she says with a smirk. "Did you tell him he was a stupid head?"

"He did," I assure her.

"It's okay," Jessie says, hugging me tightly. "We're okay."

"Better than okay," I agree, kissing the top of his head.

She smiles sincerely at us. "Good," she says with a nod. "Now that's settled, it looks like the Durhams are walking down from the house, if you want to come see what they have to say."

I raise my eyebrows and share a look with Jessie. "Oh, hell yeah," he says, tugging on my hand so we can make our way up to the closed gate.

The Durhams arrive at about the same time we do. From the look on Mrs. Durham's face, I'm guessing they've seen the contents of the leaflet themselves. Mayor Durham is holding up his palms, trying to wave us down as the crowd's booing gets louder. I notice his eyes flicking to the news camera for a fraction of a second before he plasters on a big smile for his audience. It feels as if almost everyone has their phones held up now, but the mayor isn't daunted, apparently.

"Hello, everyone," he says in a clear voice that carries through the air.

The booing dies down as I assume people want to hear whatever it is he has to say. It's easy to see why he's popular. He's classically handsome in that strong jaw, thick hair, suited and booted sort of way. But once you know he's a lying bastard with a black heart, it's a lot harder to be fooled by his appearance. As usual, his wife is dressed like a Jackie Kennedy wannabe in a light-green fitted dress suit, pearls around her neck, and white heels that are fighting her to stand still on the gravel driveway.

"I understand there are a lot of heightened emotions right now," the mayor continues. "But I assure you, this is all just a storm in a teacup."

"We didn't come down here to get gaslit by you!" the cheer captain, Lakelyn, shouts at him. Despite being half his size, she sure is fierce.

"You can't just make up stuff and play with people's lives," Candy adds.

"Yeah," Donna says with a smirk as she folds her arms. "This is called fucking around and finding out. Kids these days can discover anything on the internet if they look hard enough."

"It really wasn't that hard," someone mutters by my elbow. I turn and see Sheriff Chancey's teen girl. She flicks her eyes to me, looking worried. I give her a wink, and she grins.

Ahhhh. That makes sense now. Jessie said something about Chancey's niece being on the cheer squad. I'm assuming she teamed up with her cousin, and now here we all are.

Mayor Durham's phony smile is looking strained as more and more people start yelling at him. "There's no need for this," he's saying. "I'm sure we can straighten out these investigations with the authorities. There is nothing more important to me than this town, and I will do everything I can to keep it safe."

"You mean y'all will do everything you can to swindle votes!" an older, immaculately dressed lady shouts with a strong Texan drawl. She shakes a skillet in the direction of the Durhams, who take the smallest step back in alarm.

Mrs. Durham recovers quickly. "You should all be ashamed of yourselves!" she cries, pointing a finger out at the crowd. "My husband has run an honest campaign and kept his promises about lowering crime rates! And this is how you repay him? I think you should—"

All of a sudden, she pinwheels her arms and almost goes crashing to the ground. Her husband lunges for her, catching her necklace in the process, sending pearls flying in every direction as they immediately get lost among the stones of the driveway. As she rights herself, she lifts her left foot, showing that the heel has snapped clean off her shoe.

As people gasp, I catch a flash of movement from someone a little behind me to the left. It's that pale woman with the dark hair who Leah is so interested in. Call me crazy, but I swear I see her put a doll away in her purse that looks just like Mrs. Durham. It's like a larger version of the tiny one she snuck into Durham's own purse.

Except this one is missing its left shoe.

When she catches my eye, she raises a single finger to her black lips, and gives me a "shh" with a sly smile.

Before I can think about it too much, the sound of a car engine draws my attention, as it does many people in the crowd. I worry it's a resident. This might not be a thorough-fare, but other people do live here. However, when I crane my neck and see that it's a shiny black limousine, I figure something else might be going on.

The gentleman who steps out makes Durham look like chump change. I know nothing about fancy clothes, but his suit is obviously insanely well-tailored. I'd guess he's in his fifties with thick salt-and-pepper hair and broad shoulders. He's undoubtedly in great shape for his age, and when he throws a smile filled with perfect white teeth toward the crowd, I hear more than one person sigh wistfully.

"That's Rafferty McKenna," a young man says near us. He's got sandy blond curls and a pearl hanging from one ear. I get the impression he's a friend of Jessie's.

"The guy who owns half the town?" Jessie asks.

The young man nods but Alannah slaps her forehead and groans. "I knew I knew the name," she says, looking around at us. "He's Logan's dad."

"You know Logan McKenna?" the young man with the pearl asks in a slightly alarmed tone.

Alannah nods and looks at Jessie. "That's Tara's

boyfriend. The one who brought us the letter from the cheer board. I bet you anything he's the one who ratted you out!"

Jessie gasps, and I tighten my grip on him, tempted to give this rich asshole a piece of my mind.

"Raff, thank goodness," Durham cries as McKenna approaches the gate. McKenna, however, totally blanks him, instead slipping his hands into his pockets and addressing the crowd. He subtly makes sure the TV crew is giving him their full focus before he speaks.

"It has been brought to my attention that the current mayor of Paddle Creek has used my name and abused my good faith in an attempt to gain votes and secure his re-election. In no way do I endorse the witch hunt that has been targeting certain individuals over the past few weeks. I certainly had no idea about the accusations leveled at the mayor regarding embezzlement. Therefore, effective immediately, I will be withdrawing my endorsement of Lyle Durham as mayor in favor of Maurice Sanchez, and I will also be assisting authorities in getting to the bottom of any genuine illegal activity. Thank you."

Even though people explode with questions, he just nods once, then walks back toward his limo. "Raff!" Durham splutters, his face red and his clenched fists trembling. "You're really going to throw me under the bus like that? We had a deal! Raff!"

But McKenna slides into the back seat of his ride without acknowledging the mayor once.

"Well," Sheriff Chancey says. She's opened her car door and is standing on the edge so she's a little above the crowd as she addresses us. "I reckon I better head back into town and start working with those nice federal folks so we can close down these investigations and get you good folks back to work. Sound good?"

She's met with a thundering cheer. People clap and bang

drums and blow whistles. I turn around in time to see the Durhams scurrying back up their driveway to the safety of their house.

I can't believe what's just happened.

"Is it over?" I ask out loud, even though I'm not sure who I'm really addressing the question to. "Is that it?"

Jessie lifts my hand and kisses the backs of my fingers. "I think so," he says incredulously.

I look down at him. "But what about you? The squad, the competition."

He shrugs. "Honestly, it's okay. I don't know if there's anything that can be done."

"Oh, just you wait and see," his captain says with a savage grin on her face. "If McKenna is trying to save face, he might be willing to make that complaint disappear unless he wants his son dragged into this scandal as well."

"Damn, girl," Alannah says. "Remind me never to piss you off."

The captain winks, showing off her teal glitter. "You better believe it."

"Thank you," Jessie says, his eyes brimming with tears. "So much. You don't know what this means to me."

Lakelyn squeezes his arm. "Yes, I do, sugar."

She lets him go, and she and the rest of the cheerleaders blend into the crowd as the mood has turned celebratory. I know we don't have a permit, but I wonder if the Durhams are going to have the gall to shut down this street party. Someone starts blasting music and a bunch of the footballers offer to do a run to the liquor store.

But when Jessie turns in my arms, it's as if the entire crowd just melts away. He's all I can see.

My heart is overflowing. I regret the pain I caused him so much, but I'll never regret trying to do what I thought was best for him. I'm just so eternally grateful that it's all worked out okay and I have my kitten back in my arms.

"Please come home," I beg. "Please. Come back and never leave, Jessie."

His eyes fill with tears. "I thought maybe I'd lost you forever."

I grunt and give him a little squeeze. "That's because your Daddy is a stupid head. Sorry about that."

He leans up and kisses me sweetly. "It's okay. Do you want to make it up to me? Perhaps back in our bed?"

I grin at him. "Come to mention it, I haven't changed the sheets in *days* now."

He bites my bottom lip and drags it through his teeth. "Let's go fix that, hmm? I'm already wearing my ears, after all."

"Good kitty," I mumble against his lips, kissing him deeply.

Against the odds, I think we've made it out the other side of all this drama, and he still wants me. He still loves me.

That feels like something to celebrate.

Preferably naked and as soon as fucking possible.

Jessie

My thoughts are buzzing as we fumble our way back into the apartment. It's crazy to think that someone has so much power that they can make all the problems that have been plaguing us go away with just a few sentences spoken. But it seems like that's what's happened. I don't want to jinx anything, but there's every hope that Toe Beans is going to be okay.

I might even be allowed back on the squad, but we'll see. One thing at a time.

I know it's only been a couple of days, but I'm so relieved to be home. That this still *is* my home. Even though Nim and I are kissing like horny teenagers, we break apart, close the door, and lock the world outside. I'm delighted as several black streaks come rushing up to us, tails swishing with loud meows emanating from little bodies.

"Yes, hello!" I coo, trying to pet them all at once. "I'm home. Uncle Jessie is home! Did you look after Daddy? I bet you did. Good babies, yes, you are."

It's probably crazy that I'm thinking about bringing another cat to add to the pride, but Pisces will be my contribution, and that feels right. Nim has invited me into his home, but I want this place to become mine as well. Ours.

Besides, I'm not going to argue with a witch. If she says a cat has chosen to be mine, I believe her. No other convincing required.

I feel fingers run through my hair and look up to see Nim standing over me, beaming with such affection it takes my breath away.

"This place wasn't the same without you," he says.

I sigh happily and press my face against his palm. "My home is where you are," I tell him earnestly.

His eyes shine as he wraps his hand around my arm and encourages me to stand. Then he surprises me by sweeping me off my feet into a bridal carry. I gasp, then giggle, nuzzling my nose against his cheek.

"I think you caught a stray kitten," I tell him.

"Yes, and now he's all mine," Nim growls, kissing along my jaw. "Think I might put a collar on him and everything."

I gasp again, leaning back to study his face. Thanks to my new friendship with Kadence, I know what putting a collar on someone can mean.

It's a commitment. The forever kind.

"Do you mean it?" I whisper. My skin is hot and tingly, and there's a lump of emotion rising in my throat.

He presses a kiss to my lips then looks me deep in the eyes. "There's no rush, kitten. You've had a lot of change recently and I know we're still very new. But almost losing you made me realize how much I need you. You deserve a commitment. A promise."

I squirm in his arms, not quite believing that after feeling so low I'm getting everything I could ever dream of. "Maybe you could get me a pretty collar that I could wear for you," I say, peeking at him through my eyelashes. "Then one day…if you wanted to get me a pretty ring to match it…that would be okay."

He grins at me. "Oh, that would be okay, would it?" he teases me.

"Shut up, Daddy," I say, kissing him hard and kicking my heels in glee. "Hurry up and take me to bed already."

"Such a bossy kitty," he grumbles but his big smile somewhat diminishes any sting his words might have had.

I love that he carries me all the way into the bedroom, where he places me carefully on top of the mattress. It takes a minute to wrangle all the excitable cats out and close the door, but when we're alone, I feel electricity crackling between us as he stalks back to the bed.

He climbs on top of me, kissing me all over my face. "Let Daddy take care of you, kitten," he says. "Please."

"Thank you, Daddy," I tell him. "I love you."

"I love you *so much*, baby," he says, his voice catching. I place my hands on either side of his face and take a second to kiss him sensually. He needs to know that I believe him. But sometimes, words aren't the right thing for my grumpy Daddy with his heart of gold.

Instead, I allow him to gently pull off my cheer hoodie and the T-shirt underneath. Then I lie back with my head on a pillow, letting him unbutton my jeans and pull them down along with my underwear. Fully naked—aside from my ears that he's left on—I drape my arms above my head and watch as he undresses himself for me. Our gazes never break from each other as he drops his shirt to the floor, then shucks his pants and everything else down.

God damn it. There was a hot minute when I wondered if I'd ever see his gorgeous body again or if I'd only have my memories to keep with me. He's hard for me as he comes back to the bed and drapes himself on top of me, pressing all our delicious skin together as we kiss luxuriously. When he reaches for the nightstand, I break us apart.

"I'm okay to go bare if you are?"

He blinks at me. "Are you sure?"

We got tested together, but until now, we've still been using condoms. I think it was another way he was trying to protect me until I was ready. To be fair, I've definitely been skittish after finding out that Parker was with another man while we were together.

But I'm ready. I'm so ready to give everything to my Daddy.

"Please," I tell him, pecking a swift kiss to the tip of his nose.

His kisses are searing as he instead just picks up the lube and expertly moves us around until he's got his hand between my thighs, working my hole open with his fingers. My cock is throbbing and leaking, desperate for attention. I know that once my Daddy touches it, it'll be game over, so I let it bob over my stomach, confident it'll be worth the wait.

When Nim removes his fingers and coats his cock, ready to enter me, I place a hand on his chest, making him pause. Wordlessly, I push slightly, and he automatically follows my lead. We roll until he's on his back and I'm straddling his hips. He watches me like a hawk as I reach back and angle his length against my hole, sinking down as we both groan loudly.

"I missed you, Daddy," I whisper as I take him in deeper.

He plucks one of my hands from his chest and kisses my palm. "I'll never let that happen again," he promises me.

I know he said he wanted to take care of me, but my kitten is coming out, and I need to prove he's mine. I look down at him as he penetrates me farther, dragging my pretty manicured nails down his chest, leaving red lines that shine against his creamy skin and the dark ink of his tattoos.

"Daddy," I rasp as I bottom out, loving the fullness of him inside me. "Daddy."

"My kitten," he says, reaching up and running his thumbs over the bars in my nipples. "My beautiful boy, so good for Daddy."

I bite my lip as I start to rock. He matches me with every thrust, moving his hands down to my hips so he can steady me and control our motions. It's like I'm the center of the universe when he looks at me like that, but right now it's so much more intense than it's ever been before.

"I love you," I utter, and he gasps.

"I love you so much, kitten," he tells me back.

We pick up the pace. There will be times to take our love-making slow. But I think right now both of us need this so badly to prove that the bump in our road has long since passed. I dig my fingers into his chest as I ride him hard, my sweat dripping down onto his skin.

As predicted, as soon as he wraps his hand around my cock, I'm done. I drop my head back and scream as he jerks me off and pummels me hard. My orgasm is mind-blowing, and as I'm shooting my load all over his chest, I feel him throbbing inside me as he comes for the first time without any kind of barrier.

I tremble as my climax starts to fade, and he's immediately hugging me against him tightly, pressing his mouth everywhere it can reach. Eventually, our lips meet in a slow, sensual kiss that says so much more than words ever could.

My Daddy is never going to be a poet laureate, but that doesn't matter to me so long as he communicates the best he can. He can say everything he needs to with his mouth just like this, and I'll understand.

I am his, and he is mine. It'll be nice to have a collar and some rings to tell the world that someday. But right now, it's enough that I know it to be true.

Epilogue

Eighteen Months Later
Nim

I can't say that cheerleading competitions are my idea of a fun or relaxing time, but it's always worth it to see my baby boy shine on that big blue mat.

I'll be forever grateful that Rafferty McKenna was able to undo whatever damage his son did and get Jessie's name cleared with the Cheer First cheerleading association. I don't know what strings he pulled, and honestly, I probably don't want to know. The bottom line is that Jessie wasn't punished because of me, and he was allowed to pursue his dream of college cheer.

The team welcomed him back with open arms. Apparently, the girl dating McKenna's son left in a big fit of dramatics, taking her nasty little cronies with her. That meant that Jessie's best friend, Alannah, could join the competition squad like she always wanted, so I think it all worked out for the best.

I've been to every one of their competitions so far, and

I've been so proud watching them flourish, aware of how much Jessie poured his heart and soul into their training. It was no surprise to me that when he entered his sophomore year, he earned a place on the committee.

And now here we are in Nashville at the Kittens' first grand national championship in years. I'm watching the current team with butterflies in my stomach, knowing that my boy is going to hit the mat next.

When the Kittens needed to raise the funds to pay for entry fees, transportation, and accommodation, the Cardinals were the first to come forward and offer to help with fundraising. We held an event at O'Toole's as a thank-you for the way the cheerleaders all came together and saved our community when we thought all hope was lost.

Mercifully, the temporary closure didn't affect Toe Beans too badly in the end. In fact, thanks to all the media coverage at our protest, as soon as I opened the doors again, we were booked up for months in advance. We were able to survive those couple of low-income months because of the boom that followed. I didn't have to lose any staff. Actually, I soon had to hire more.

More importantly than that, though, was that the applications for cat adoptions doubled. It's been a year and a half, and we're still rotating through cats at record speed as more and more fur babies find their forever homes.

Speaking of which, Jessie and I did indeed end up with an eleventh black cat at home. However, thanks to the café's increased popularity, even the new black cats have been finding homes. At Jessie's insistence, I got Leah to do a special series of videos about how black cats are always the last to be picked, and people took that to heart. So for now, at least, it seems like we're stopping at eleven.

Thank goodness. We ran out of star signs, after all.

As soon as we reopened, the very first adoption was from

Sheriff Chancey. It was obvious to me that she bonded with the feisty tabby kitty, who she promptly named McNulty after her favorite TV detective, and I was glad to see him go to someone who I knew to be loyal and protective. Besides, if she hadn't taken him, I was in real danger of doing it myself.

Eleven cats is a *lot* for one apartment, however. Which is why since Christmas, Jessie and I have started house hunting. I'll miss living right above the café, but the new home we've found is only a ten-minute drive away and has about triple the square feet. So much more room for all of us, especially as I'm planning on making a massive catio so our fur babies can safely explore outside.

Having Jessie move in with me right from the start felt like the universe telling us to be together despite our reservations. But it was always my place that Jessie adapted to. The new home will be all ours, together. I can't wait for that.

The current team finishes their routine with a flourish, and the crowd cheers, bringing my attention back to the here and now. I clap politely, but my eyes automatically flick to the side of the stage, anxious to get a glimpse of my baby before he goes on. I'm standing with a bunch of other friends and family members of the Kittens, several of us wearing some kind of purple and teal combination. I'm rather brazenly sporting a T-shirt that reads KITTEN DADDY that Jessie got for me as a joke but I'm surprising him by actually wearing it today. I know he'll be absolutely thrilled.

Since our hiccup near the start of the relationship, I try my best to always go out of my way to show him how treasured he is and how proud I am that he's mine. He has a collection of collars now ranging from simple chokers to ones with proper leather straps. The only time he doesn't wear them is when he's training, performing, or competing, as it could be dangerous. Instead, he's got a sheet of temporary tattoos in the shape of paws, and he puts one on if there's an audience. That way, we both know that he's telling people he's someone's kitten, even if nobody else knows it.

A familiar face pops out from behind the curtain, scanning the crowd. My heart leaps, and I thrust my arm into the air to wave. As soon as he sees me, his face breaks into a breathtaking smile, and I'm sure I grin like a lunatic. He gives me a little wave back and blows a kiss before disappearing again, no doubt to get his head in the game.

I keep waiting for the day when I'm not dazed by just the mere sight of him, but it certainly hasn't come yet.

The announcer's magnified voice comes over the sound system once more. "On deck, please welcome…the Paddle! Creek! Kittens!"

I bellow my lungs out as the team runs and flips their way onto the mat, waving at the crowd as they take their place. They all look down with their arms by their sides, waiting for the chaotic, fast-paced music to start.

Just before it does, I see Jessie glance up and catch my eye, giving me a wink, letting me know that he might be up there with the team, but he'll be performing just for me.

My baby boy. The best kitten a Daddy could ever ask for, even if he fell into my lap by accident.

They say that cats have nine lives. I hope Daddies do as well.

Because I plan on spending every single one of them with Jessie.

———

Thank you so much for reading **Nim and Jessie's** story! If you enjoyed their kitty adventure, please leave a review on your favorite bookish site. It makes a big difference for us indie authors!

If you want to find out how Jessie's friend Kadence

develops an unlikely relationship with billionaire Rafferty McKenna, make sure you pre-order **Paddle Creek Daddies #6: Make Believe** now! Out April 2024.

Turn the page to discover more heartwarming Daddy books by Helen Juliet/HJ Welch including all the previous Paddle Creek Daddies books.

———

Thank you to my team!

Cover Design: Cate Ashwood

Editing: Meg Cooper

Proof Reading: Tanja Ongkiehong

Special thanks: Troo for the awesome plot suggestions!

Love and support: Ed, Rena, Hubby, and our cats

to my rescue. Maybe what me and these god-like men have isn't just a fling after all?

Heaven Sent is a steamy, standalone MMM romance. It's the first book in the **Paddle Creek College** series, where it's always the quiet ones who get up to the best kind of trouble. This book features a geek tutoring two hot jocks, two hot jocks tutoring a geek in a completely different way, a trash panda with a heart of gold, a human ice cream sundae, a revenge curse, and a guaranteed HEA with absolutely no cliffhanger.

Click here to get the Heaven Sent eBook

Also Available

Paddle Creek Daddies #2: Yes, Sir by HJ Welch

Two men. Two secrets. Can true love set them free?

BENEDICT

Just one more year, then I can go back to my beloved Oxford University and leave this tiny town behind me. Teaching is my passion, but I have other desires that I know would get me fired if anyone found out. The only trouble is, my new TA is pushing all my buttons and I'm not sure he even realizes what calling me Sir does to me. That's nothing, however, compared to when he starts calling me Daddy.

JACKSON

Have I got hots for teacher? Oh, yes. Messing around is off the table, though, so in a way it's safe to flirt with him and see him lose that stiff upper lip. It's not like he'd be interested in me anyway if he ever discovered what I love wearing under my clothes. Tough guys like me shouldn't like satin and lace. They shouldn't want to feel pretty. But Sir makes me feel gorgeous, and I want to be *such* a good boy for him.

***Yes, Sir** is a steamy, standalone MM romance. It's the second book in the **Paddle Creek College** series, where it's always the quiet ones who get up to the best kind of trouble. This book features two people learning they don't have to be ashamed of who they are, a sassy brat who really wants to behave, a master in the bedroom who's a caring Daddy at heart, role playing so good it could win an Oscar, and a guaranteed HEA with absolutely no cliffhanger.*

Click here to get the Yes, Sir eBook

boy to his inner little, the most loyal doggy best friend, a lot of dinosaurs, a heart-stopping rescue, and a guaranteed HEA with absolutely no cliffhanger. CW: Age play but no ABDL.

Click here to get the Little Pleasures eBook

Click here to get the Four Play eBook

Click here to get the bonus short story Be Four

fabulous, too bright and beautiful for shy little me, so I've never said a word. However, something strange starts happening the more time we spend with our new friend, Andreas. The older man gives the most amazing cuddles and can't seem to stop showering me and Jalen with gifts. Traveling to England feels like something from a fairy tale, but what's even more unbelievable is the way his eyes light up when he's with me and my best friend. Am I crazy? Could three really be the magic number?

***Jalen & Colby** is part of A Daddy for Christmas, a multi-author series. All the books are standalones, but each Daddy has a unique gift for his wonderful boy (or boys). Except all boys know that sometimes Santa gets it wrong, and it's going to take a very special Daddy to make it right. So why not stay and read them all?*

some by the end of the year, they don't expect to all fall for the same gorgeous, slightly scary-looking Daddy. The only solution? Let him choose who he wants to bed. Except he doesn't. Daddy Wolf wants to spoil each little piggy, one after another. But when danger comes calling, will their love for each other be enough to save them all?
Includes Halloween bonus scene!

Nine Lives

When Charlie suddenly finds himself homeless and penniless, he decides to sell the only thing left he owns. Himself. For the very first time. Lucky for him he stumbles across Miller, the own of a London kink club, who saves him from those who would take advantage of him. As Miller discovers his inner Daddy, he also unlocks Charlie's kitten alter-ego. But with both their families meddling, will new love be enough to keep them together?

Click here to get the Daddy's Fairy Tales Box Set

About the Author

HJ Welch is a British author of contemporary American MM small town series and books in multi authored shared universes, including the international number one bestselling Homecoming Hearts. She lives just outside of London with her husband and three balls of fluff that occasionally pretend to be cats.

She began writing at an early age, later honing her craft online in the world of fanfiction on sites like Wattpad. Fifteen years and over half a million words later, she sought out original MM novels to read. By the end of 2016 she had written her first book of her own, and in 2017 she achieved her lifelong dream of becoming a full-time author.

When she's not writing she's usually dancing, singing, filming music videos, taking long walks, working on jigsaw puzzles, drinking prosecco, or talking about Eurovision.

She also writes contemporary British MM fairy tale adaptation as Helen Juliet, including bestsellers Thorn in His Side, A Right Royal Affair, and Three.

———

You can contact Helen via the following:
Newsletter: https://www.subscribepage.com/helenjuliet
Website – www.hjwelch.com
Facebook Group – Helen's Jewels
Instagram – @helenjwrites

Twitter – @helenjwrites
Book Bub – @HJWelchAuthor
Facebook Page – @HJWelchAuthor

www.ingramcontent.com/pod-product-compliance
Lightning Source LLC
Chambersburg PA
CBHW060711190726
48289CB00002B/634